I'M JAYME

SUSAN PEPPER ROBBINS

For information contact:
Unsolicited Press
Portland, Oregon
www.unsolicitedpress.com
orders@unsolicitedpress.com
619-354-8005

Cover Art: Jordan Pepper
Cover Design: Kathryn Gerhardt
Editor: S.R. Stewart

ISBN: 978-1-956692-72-3

CHAPTER 1

"Fall down and break your neck!" Jayme is yelling inside her head. Then she whispers JK. Sometimes she yells at her dead brother Jimmy, "It's a shit house here. WTF. I miss you. I need you, you deadbeat, faker. You One and Done. Did you drive into that tree on purpose? I think you did just to get away from what I have to deal with."

Sometimes Jayme wishes the virus would take them all out together, maybe to be with Jimmy in a nice quiet place.

She knows she is one step away from a shrink who'd advise some wilderness school where she would have to learn advanced survival skills. Or die. No phones allowed. No rescues. No Wi-Fi, not that it's reliable here. She'd go now. Maybe Montana where the virus is shooting people like a drunk movie cowboy. She needs those killer skills, people skills. She already can deal with rivers and trees, wild dogs and coyotes. The wilderness stuff would be easy. It's the still alives, the old humans, her grandparents and their son, her dad--they call "Son"-- and their divorced daughter-in-law, her mom, who wants her and everyone to call her Helen. Yes, all four of the still-alives need killing. JK. Five if she counts herself. She'd heard about an attorney who killed, they think, five people and who told the prison shrink that "they'd needed killing." She has a flash of understanding of that killer. JK, she says to herself.

It's her dad and her divorced mom Jayme has the most trouble with. It's good that there is not enough money to send her out West to get "adjusted." Who knew that no money was a good thing, and is keeping her from being sent to a wilderness place to learn how to live with "challenges," the brochure said.

Virginia has its own challenges. Unreliable connections to the internet, a dead brother, a dad who lives in his own space, a mom who is hyper, grandparents who are on the way out, a boyfriend who says he wants to be more than a friend. He means, of course, sex.

But if she were sent away, she'd hate to give up on Neal, who is not her boyfriend in the sense that most people mean, and that he hopes will happen. He was away at a fancy ass boarding school and is a year older, and now he's headed to the University.

Jayme thinks she knows almost all she needs to know. She does know plenty but not everything. Still, Jayme likes her confidence in herself, in her own opinions. Sometimes she says to herself about sex, "Not yet," and sometimes, "Dream on." Sometimes she thinks she and Neal are both playing a long game. Who will hold out the longest? That is live through the long miserable time of being young. Neal has said to her that sex is not impossible during Covid, the plague. They are friends with no benefits or privileges. They talk about sex, doing it, but haven't tried it. They have facetime, but with the flickering Wi-Fi, there's not much of that. They both laugh because they have only kissed, each time remembered exactly by Jayme and probably not at all, she thinks, by Neal. She hopes someday to ask him if he does remember.

She had put her fingers, smoky from the barbecued venison she burnt on the fire she had made, the deer she had killed with one shot thinking Neal and her dad would be impressed. This is the last weekend he was home from his fancy prep school Belmont and then he is off to a full ride at the University as an Echols Scholar who gets to take the courses he wants to.

Jayme had seen three doe and shot her arrow at a turkey but missed. The arrow was lost in the thicket. Fifty dollars gone. That night had been one of kisses.

Neal had told her how to make the fire flare up and make the meat sizzle even though it was so lean with little fat to drip and sizzle. Neal knows a lot, but from books she tells him. She knows things from the woods and fields. She had laughed and said they could have eaten faster if they'd used her grandmother's kitchen, not the ring of rocks and the wood fire with the old cast iron frying pan with no lid. It was good he knew how to make a fire from the internet and she knew how to shoot from practicing.

Her mom calls her dad her "first husband," thinking it's modern and cool, but it's not. Parents get things wrong but don't know it. No need to yell the facts she has to live with.

"Shut up and live," Neal tells her is his motto. "Go to the University. Get a job. Grow up." Sometimes he sounds a hundred years old. That's why, probably, he is always on Gram's and Joe's sides, no matter what. Not that she would ever admit it or show it, but that is one reason, one of several that Jayme thinks she will marry Neal. She has told him and he's available.

She, part of her, really wants Gram who calls her Jimmy to fall down the steps though Covid would be more natural. She's sick of her. She is sick and tired of hearing what amazes her Gram: "dinosaurs became birds!" This came from the Nature show on Wednesday nights. She is sick of her life at her house with her dad who has the stupid nickname of "Son" because he's still a "son" to Gram and Grampa Joe, even though he's forty and divorced. "So, he's left with one dead son and me left over alive," Jayme says out loud for nobody's benefit. No need to yell the facts she has to live with. Neal is right, just shut up.

Maybe the virus will take them all out. Everyone is pretending to be another person, living on another planet. They don't need masks. They never take theirs off, the invisible ones, the ones they generate from deep inside the engines of their personal histories to hide behind, and they don't think the virus is as bad as the reports make it seem. Not that they are Trumpers, just their regular selves pretending they are fine. The virus isn't real. Not a killer. Just a little version of the flu. No one wears a real mask except as a kind of costume for special occasions. Jayme suspects Gram does not really have dementia. She is pretending she's crazy for what reason, Jayme is not sure. Maybe her Gram wants to preserve or to build her own world again where a grandson did not run into a tree, the big oak in the curve on Sawmill Road, the one they all knew was a killer, Dead Man's Curve on the stretch past Sports Lake. Dementia is her mask and it helps her be the sweet granny type, the person she was before

Covid. And it hides her grief for her dead grandson from herself.

Jayme is collecting facts that tell her that Gram does not have Lewy Body Dementia. She must have learned that weird name from a book or maybe from Google though she pretends she does not know how to turn on the computer, but how does she know that the chardonnay she drinks every night at nine o'clock has more arsenic in it than any other wine.

"Arsenic and old lace," she says, toasting the life they now are living without Jimmy. She still has Son and Jayme and Grandpa Joe. She pretends—thanks to her mask—that Helen is still married to Son. She tries to still live in her classroom where she taught freshmen English called Rhetoric at the old college—too old and too rich to fail or even go to online classes. She must have been asked to retire by the dean because she told him she couldn't teach writing on Zoom. She pretends that she didn't "retire" which sounds more dignified and deliberate. No, she "resigned" she explains to anyone who will listen even though she says in a sweet demented way, apologizing for going on and on because she knows, she says, how tedious explanations are. She has gone on and on to Jayme when she is helping her put on her garden shoes, about how she had resigned to protest going virtual, having online classes, zoomed learning. It was a foolish and wasted gesture because the online world, the cyber universe was the new reality, and she was the one left behind, out of step, but she goes on and on telling how she had told the dean about how she felt and how he had said he understood, but she would have to resign or as he put it kindly, retire.

Jayme is not sympathetic and hopes she won't have to hear the explanation again, but she is sure she will. Helen says that Gram jumped ship before it sank or she thought it was sinking, but Gram says she was forced to walk the plank. Who cares, Jayme yells.

It's strange that Gram's biscuits are the same as always, her garden is weeded and watered perfectly. The kitchen never has dirty dishes though she says it does. The evidence of being in her right mind betrays her. She is not demented except when it suits her. Maybe it is a smart thing to do to avoid what's going on or has gone on—the death of Jimmy, the divorce of Son and Helen, the drinking, Jayme's silence/her bad attitude, her own resignation/retirement/ walked plank/jumped ship.

Jayme knows she is not a good granddaughter, not a good person, not even a good girlfriend, not even a wannabe girlfriend. She wishes she could put on a mask—the recruited point guard, the high scorer on the SAT's, the cool girl. Instead she looks like what Neal teases her that she looks like--"the serial killer," then adds "maybe just a Becky" but goes on to say that it's clear that she likes the look and laughs when she says, "Kill me now." He wants to go to law school so looking like a SK or having a girlfriend who looks like one will bring him clients, even if many will be court appointed. "At first," he laughs again.

Jayme's dad, "Son," pretends he is still a teenager and her mom, Helen, pretends that she is still married and visits her former in-laws and tells them what she wants them to do about their medicine and doctors' appointments and they pretend to listen and take her advice. Helen pretends to take an interest in the day-to-day life Jayme lives as a senior in high school, but Jayme is as sure as fire that the one thing her mom really cares about is her grades which she says determine what her future will be. So far, Jayme is Honor Roll perfect. "Be any kind of doctor or lawyer," she says to Jayme, trying to make it sound like a joke, but it's serious. Helen likes to think of herself as a person who tells the truth, but it's hard when her whole universe is crazy-- not being what it used to be—halfway normal.

Jayme feels that she is living in a house where nothing is what or who it seems to be or should be or used to be. Maybe the furniture is—the kitchen table is itself. Gram uses old slang as if she were a girl again. Jayme is "Angel Cake" or "Dream Beam" but "A Bomb" is the name that seems to fit Jayme best. She might go off, explode or do something criminal. She doesn't trust herself all the time.

Gram stumbles, then Jayme feels bad. Gram is so out of it or pretends she is. When she says she loves to talk about people behind their backs, she really means that she is telling only good things about them. She reverses things and it drives Jayme crazy. If Jayme tripped Gram or pushed her down the steps, she would whisper that Jayme was so athletic and graceful!

Recently, Gram has been saying "Whatever." And she likes the sound of "social distancing." She is distanced from everything, but is happy in her faked Alzheimered way, if it is faked. She calls it being happy in a new kind of way which makes Jayme suspect that she does know what's what and how their world has changed—not only because of the damn virus, as Son always calls it, but because of Jimmy's death and then the divorce of Jimmy and Jayme's parents.

Gram is determined, Jayme feels, to find something to be happy about in what's left of the old world when things meant what they meant. BCV. Before Corona Virus. Black people's lives always mattered more than white people admitted but now things were worse for everyone. Black Lives Mattered in the slave economy of the South her favorite teacher, Mr. Carver, says, more than white lives in many ways. Someone in the back of the class had yelled, "NO, Property Matters!"

Crazy as it all is, Gram is the one person who understands Jayme's stuttering, and who says she does not have a "speech impairment." She told the doctors who diagnosed it the same thing when Jayme was four. Now, at sixteen, going on seventeen as the old song says, she is almost free of it, and can even give an oral book report back when they had regular, real, face to face classes, not online fake classes. Only when she thinks about sad things, does the stutter, "the brown dog," she calls it, return and then it is a hesitation, some longer than others. Maybe when she is pretending that life is good on any terms. Zoomed, but good. In the Cloud, but good.

She takes four steps at a time up to where Gram is standing, smiling. Crouching her almost six feet, one hundred twenty-three pounds over her, Jayme holds her high under her arms so tight she can feel Gram's heart beating against her wrists. They come slowly down the staircase that turns twice at right angles. She hates her for singing "Here

Comes the Bride." As a kid, she always sang back, "I am the goon."

As always, Gram says, "Thank you, Jimmy."

Jayme answers, "I'm Jayme, Gram."

Jimmy is deader than dead. The movie of it runs through Jayme's head whenever it wants to. Last spring, his 1953 V-8 Ford pick-up ran off the road into an oak tree. When he didn't come home by 2:00 a.m., Son called Jimmy's girlfriend, Holly, hoping he'd fallen asleep at her house, but no, Jimmy had left her in the middle of Colbert to get home early so he could get up early to go turkey hunting. Jayme had been all set to go with him. They loved to see the gobblers blow up into a ball of white feathers and hurl themselves back into the early spring woods, strutting and drumming, spitting, their long, six-inch blood red beards hanging down as they looked for hens. Hunting turkeys would give them, Jimmy had said, a good start before the long day of cutting grass at the cemetery and golf course. Jayme believed everything Jimmy said, but that was then and now was now. Jayme did not believe anything much now.

One gobbler a day, reported on the cell phone. One day at a time, one hour at a time. "Don't jump ahead," the grief counselor had said to her. "Baby steps."

No one thought of the back road short cut that Jimmy had taken until the next day at noon. At the curve, the oak tree grew almost in the road, and the road crew took five hours to get Jimmy's truck—the pieces of it—hauled away. It was raining and the fenders were crumpled and glistening. Water ran off them like they had just come through the car wash. Jayme thought she saw Jimmy wedged under the dash, looking surprised, but dead. She knew she was hallucinating.

Wrecked people look worse than regular dead people, Jayme was sure. She had seen five dead people—two cancers, one stroke, two old ages.

After Jimmy's wreck, Jayme and her dad moved in with Gram and Joe. Helen had said she needed to be by herself. Helen said grieving was selfish and it was a private matter and suited only for conversation with a counselor or maybe a pastor. It was a bad move in every way. Gram had hardening of the arteries and Joe stayed slightly lit. By then, six months "After-the-Wreck," as they all called Jimmy's death, there was a divorce in the works for Son and Helen. Helen had never moved in, not even for one night,

But Helen comes to visit all the time. Son just looks at her. He never speaks to her except through Jayme. "Ask your mother if you need a physical before school starts."

Helen is saying to Jayme, "We've tried, darling, God knows and you know too, how hard it has been to make it work. Your dad and I were wrong for each other and too young when we got married. I was exactly your age when I met Son. Don't you even look at anyone until you are twenty-five? Tell that young man from Belmont School to get lost. We have to make this divorce work for your sake and mine too. For your father too." Helen looks like an old teenager in her shaggy hair and Levi's. She is thirty-five.

"You've been to another one of those stupid, jerk hole support groups, Jayme says. "They ruin the way you say things."

"You should come to the next one. It's on relating to parents, divorced parents, as people," Helen says.

"God knows I've tried that," Jayme says as she slices the Velveeta for Joe. It's one of the few things Joe can eat, but he hates it and asks for sharp, black rind cheese every time. Jayme has stopped explaining to Joe that he can't eat it. "All of you, except Gram maybe, are people instead of parents. Too much people. Not one parent in the bunch of you."

Jayme's boyfriend, Neal, is not a forever thing, but he pretends he is. He loves her because she never pretends and it is like having cold water thrown in his face, in a good way. Here's what she told him the last time she had time to talk to him. Off at a private boarding school, as Neal is, Jayme likes having "a rich un-redneck boyfriend," not that she thinks of Neal exactly as her boyfriend, more like her what? Squire? Her vassal, her servant. In her last phone call, her usual monologue, she went on and on which he said he loved and said he was saving it to replay over and over. She thinks she never pretends but sometimes it is pleasant to go along with what other people want to be true. Here's the message he saved from her:

"When I was called a white bitch at school, a Karen, I say back that's racist. Reversed racism. That shuts people down for a while and then we don't speak and go about our business. Or, then I am never spoken to or even looked at again. Of course I do care. I try to always tell the truth and when I am accused of being mean, bitchy, I say, that's right. I am and want to be or have to be.

I have a boyfriend, that's you, Neal. My family is dysfunctional, calls me Jimmy, my brother as you know who was killed in a wreck last year. I am surprised when you told me I was going to marry you but not right away. That was when I had just met you, but I warned you it would not be until you take the bar exam. I am glad to have an almost lawyer boyfriend. You are not a redneck, but you wish you were. You are very smart and you have relatives who have been to jail. That's cool I think and wish that some of mine had been caught. I'd go to see them because that's also who I am, a good person.

In the world we live in, someone has to tell it the way it is. What it is. I am glad to have you as my boyfriend. You are tall and smart. I am very tall, very blonde and many say I am beautiful. I don't think so, but I have read that beautiful women don't see themselves as beautiful and are always finding fault with themselves, skin, hair, weight."

CHAPTER 2

Now Jayme is sure the iPhone she bought from Scott was stolen. Scott had "found" it; he said what he sold were "found objects." Scott's sense of humor is as weird as his looks. One pierced ear with a wire hanging out with a turquoise drop on the end. His tats are all, he says, Art Deco. And for twenty bucks, Jayme jumped for one between her ring finger and pinkie. Scott says he wishes he were African American because he would take advantage of being seen as a victim of white people. It's a crazy thing to think and the Black kids tell him he doesn't know what he's talking about. They laugh at or ignore him but he still shows up at all their parties. "I don't have to be invited. I count on the superior manners of the Black culture. They learned grace from being slaves. Who wouldn't learn how to defer to power? I can explain this if anyone is interested." No one is. Occasionally, Scott has something interesting to say that shows sympathy for groups that don't usually get any—slave owners or rich people. Their souls are deformed but in ways we dismiss because it seems we are excusing their crimes, but we aren't. Studies are made of killers and rapists and other evil doers but the scholars are not seen as supporting or justifying the crimes. Slave owners and any kind of corporate stakeholder are not looked at with any sympathy. No one listens to him when he goes on. Neal tells him he sounds like and is racist, and Scott answers that racists need a better analysis, maybe their cruel parents, the usual suspects.

When Jayme tells Gram this about Scott, she is surprised that Gram says she understands completely, but adds that Scott is on dangerous ground, insulting Black Americans and also white people who take offense at such "appropriation." Gram points out how insulting it is for people to say they know how she feels about losing her grandson. You don't like for old people to pretend to be young, use the slang or dance the dances, or know the music.

"Like Helen does all the time," Jayme says under her breath, but Gram hears her and smiles a little... Gram has depths that Jayme admires even though they drive her crazy, so she ignores them.

"Still, I'm your basic good ole boy," Scott loves to say as he listens to what she says. He eats in the English style, plastering food on the back of the fork with his knife, and using his knife constantly. Jayme thinks Scott likes to have a knife in his hand as much as is possible.

"My origins are humble; my Ma was good looking, the last time I saw her; my old man should have been rich, but someday not too far off from now, I'll be.

Scott likes Joe. Their mean streaks, admitted and enjoyed, made them look like friends in the yellow plastic yard chairs in the back of the house with azaleas and boxwood. "As usual, Gram did it backwards. The vegetables should have been put in the back of the house, the useless boxwood and azaleas in the front," Joe says to Scott who grins.

Scott approves of Neal who takes the pressure off him to be the boyfriend. Plus Neal was away at Belmont.

Gram had taught Rhetoric for years. She would explain to anyone who'd listen that the word was a Greek word, an ancient one for persuasion," but Jayme wasn't ever sure of that. Joe didn't help when he said it was all Greek to him. When she looked at him, he snarled "Amo, Amas Amat." Gram would laugh and say sweetly, "Latin, Silly." Scott loved to get them started. Jayme felt like it sometimes herself but didn't feel right when Scott felt free to crank them up.

"Her gardens are as nutty as she is," Joe tells Scott.

"Yes sir," Scott replies agreeably.

"Takes one to know one," Jayme adds, trying to horn in on the friendliest pair she's seen at Brookwood since Jimmy's wreck.

"Show some respect," Joe directs at Jayme a bourbon-y goofball smile. It seems all right for outsiders to joke about the nuts in the family but family can't. It's supposed to be the other way around, Jayme thinks.

Joe has a mean streak, no doubt about it. He taught Jimmy and Jayme their ABC's out of order. Jimmy had to repeat first grade, and Jayme had to go to summer "camp" which meant summer school, in order to pass into the second grade. "Slow starters," they were called, but Joe had had his hand in the slow start. Jimmy had caught up by the fourth grade and been honor roll from then on.

Scott is telling Joe his Smurf joke.

"How do Smurfs make love?" he asks Joe who pushes his cigarette down into the black dirt around the boxwood and puts his slippered foot on the little green fence around the shrub, bending it.

"What's a damn Smurf?" Joe wants to know.

"They smuck," Scott laughs at Joe's question.

"Get it, Joe, Smuck?" Jayme asks Joe.

"Nothing to get," says Joe.

Jayme is embarrassed, but she can see what Joe meant. "Nothing to get, was the way she was beginning to feel about Scott, what he had to say and what he had to sell that he had "found."

Scott sold everything from pills for the Coronavirus, he called it the C-thing, medicine which was, in fact, over the counter blood pressure pills that make you a little light headed. His book reports that he cobbled together from the internet went for twenty-five dollars. He had a file of term papers for all classes—Voc. Ed. To A.P. History. Jimmy had given him his ten-pager "The Role of the Hessian Mercenaries in the Revolutionary War" and had refused the hundred dollars in twenties Scott had offered. Jimmy had known Scott had a buyer who wanted it—it had gotten an A—and was willing to fork over two hundred fifty. Jimmy knew what was what. Scott had science projects for sale too, and was working on a catalog of his "resources and products" he called them. What he did for free was turkey hunting videos and some day he would have a web page selling the camo outfits, the cameras, the guns, maybe even recipes of turkey breasts grilled with basil, lemon and sea salt.

Joe, even with his mean streak, was a man who picked the wild plums and blackberries that grew in the ditches along the roads. No other men that Jayme knew did things like that. Joe looked like the codgers in the old Foxfire books, churning, whittling and making whiskey and soap.

Neal, always on Jayme's horizon, but far off, too cool to call except when there was not much else to do. "Not yet," Jayme said to put herself to sleep, "Not yet."

Neal's father, more typical of "the world in which we live today," another of Jayme's school phrases, had gotten a permanent at the village Beauty Salon, but he thought picking fruit the way Joe did was woman's work. Probably would have said, "Fruits for the fruit," or something semi-cute.

"You're lucky your dad doesn't get a perm. It is so embarrassing," Neal told Jayme.

"Yeah, but I've got a Son for a Dad. Top that."

"Another unusual thing about Joe was that he read books and listened to music from Bach to Oompah to Kendrick Lamar. He put a slate roof on the dogs' houses, but let them sleep in the house which he pointed out had a damned asbestos roof of paper. Joe was getting worse. His ankles were swollen at night and sometimes he let Jayme soak his feet. Jayme had to fill the pan and dump it. She knew it irritated Joe to have her dripping water and lifting his heavy feet into the pan, but he let Jayme cut the thick toenails with the nail cutter. Joe could hardly eat now, just the little gobs of Velveeta.

"Can you blame me?" He was looking at the plate of burned sausages and apples Gram had tried to cook after

Della left for the day. Helen had hired Della Trenholm to come in every day to get things straightened out. Joe sometimes answered the unasked questions with the question. "Got any more of the Velveeta?"

Della is Black, but sometimes she is African American, "depending on the circumstances and the location." She tells Jayme what's what about the "Black-White connections in the county. Her degree is in business and she goes to all the school board meetings. What she says is weightier in its omissions and implications than in its "content. "White people do not always know what they mean or how wrong they are and were. My great-grandfather was a slave right where you live, on what used to be a farm and now is a few acres. I know you can't help any of all that history. Me either. We have to live now and I appreciate the little bit of money your dad pays me for being kind to his mama which I want to be anyway and would be kind for free if I could afford it, but I have Ricky, my burden of a grand boy who dropped out of your class for no reason except that it drove him crazy to see how things went there. White kids spoiled rotten and black kids blamed or corrected, not in the open, but still…Della knows about how the rich man who owned Sears had built schools for black children during the bad times, and she knows how some of her cousins were sent away when the county closed the public schools. She prays for Ricky who has a dangerous temper. She expects the worst and hopes for/prays for the best. She has stories about her relatives who lived, she always adds, "survived" on Pocahontas Island, not as slaves, but free. "Of course, we had slaves around here. Their graves are all over the woods."

Jayme feels that she is seeing the world up close and loves her talks with Della when Gram is having a nap. Della raised another grandson, Amar, who went to college "on football." He loves the game and what it's doing for him. Della laughs and says, "Football is helping us all."

"Night falls on Brookwood," Jayme said.

"I know I'm lucky to have some Velveeta in the refrigerator," she told Neal on the phone that night. He laughed as if he knew all that it meant. Jayme loved him for thinking he understood what she said. Maybe he did a little, Neal who had never made a sandwich for anyone else in his life.

"I'll be his first to have one he makes, I bet." Jayme tries not to talk to herself.

CHAPTER 3

Son was cooking. His idea of supper was homemade pizza. The crust was from a box. He layered crumbled sausage and hamburger, onions, cheese, peppers, hot dogs, pickles and anchovies.

"Pickle Pizza?" Jayme asks, carefully mild in her best basic daughter voice.

"Anchovies are pickled fish," Son says, his head lowered into the oven arranging the onions again on the pizza.

"Is pizza what Joe and Gram should eat?"

"Can't hurt them."

"They sure eat it, anyway," Jayme says the right thing. Son smiles.

Helen's idea of supper was broiled red snapper at the Top of the Tower, spinach salad and ice cream with crème de menthe poured on it. She took Jayme there for her birthday in September.

"Tastes like cough syrup and ruins the ice cream."

"Really," said her mother. "You'll learn, I hope. There are finer things."

She means finer than Son offers. Living with Helen, Jayme feels she'd turn into a teen model type, underfed.

She'd call vegetables "veggies" and think they belonged in salad bars.

Jimmy, like Son, could cook. Jimmy could, in fact, do anything. Even help Gram dress. Since The Wreck, without Jimmy, she wears things wrong side out, unzipped and backwards.

Jayme hates to see Gram's stomach attached to her like a misplaced buttock, her varicose veins and purple ankles. She smells old, even after she or Della has bathed and powdered her. Jimmy used to tease Gram to get her into support hose and real dresses, not the house coats she wears now. "Shimmy, Gram, Hit it, Shove it," he used to yell as he helped her. Like dead brothers in stories and movies, Jimmy was the good one, Jayme thought. M.V.P. on the school's team, straight B pluses without Scott's help, 1410 on his SAT's.

Jayme's algebra II had come out D minus, which meant tutoring last summer. Not in algebra but in study skills. She wondered if any of the tutors really knew algebra. All the one-on-one tutors seemed to know was how to *plan* to study, how to "SQ3R: Scan, Question, Read, 'Rite and Review." They gave quizzes on how to study instead of how to work word problems or equations. Son was shelling out two hundred dollars for three weeks of SQ3R.

Jayme's history ended up C plus, English C minus, and Art, a joke course, a B.

Scott made straight A's and said, "No wonder, with my resources." Scott's advice, free, was to get tough with Gram. Scott's toughness was the kind that set up match pyres for baby mice and burned them as he watched steadily, at least, he said he watched... Scott would definitely ignore an old flake of a woman, or make fun of her, leaning down the steps calling for her dead grandson, "Jimmy, Jimmy." She was delighted when Jayme showed up. "Hi, Jimmy," she'd say and Jayme would answer, "No, not Jimmy. I'm Jayme."

"You spend too much time with her," Scott said to Jayme, "your grades suffer."

Scott left a great deal to be desired, as Helen would say. Jayme realized that she was beginning to talk and think like Gram and Helen. It was sickening to feel their phrases type themselves across her brain. Without being what her chronological age demanded, wild, or, she tried to refuse to think, in Helen's words, without "sowing wild oats," she had become in Gram's phrase, a "stick in the mud."

"I've skipped my youth. Kill me now. Slay me." Jayme says to herself in the hall mirror, even though she knew she was using "slay" wrong. "And Gram's a bride again every time she comes down the steps. She's double dipping in youth. Joe can't or won't lift a finger for her and Son is too caught up in his own forty year old 'mid-life crisis' as Helen calls it."

"Men go through the equivalent of what women do when menopause hits, only it's worse, more dramatic, as usual," Helen had explained the divorce to Gram. "They go crazy around forty."

Gunning her Honda 250 XL, another purchase from Scott who swore he got it for peanuts from the impounded lot sale, Jayme heads for the shed to see how Joe is coming with the blade for the lawnmower. He is slowly filing the blade held in the vise. He looks amused and idiotic, but his strokes are sure and steady. He hasn't mentioned or noticed, maybe, Jayme's buzzing up to the three calves. Son is lot feeding them for the veal market. Fresh manure splatters on the Honda's fender and Jayme's jeans. Three calves on seven acres. It's a cartoon farm; ridiculous, she thinks.

"Shit on a shit," Jayme yells to the calves. They look at her agreeably.

Son wanted Jayme and Jimmy to call him Son, not Dad. "Because," he explained to Jayme, "I was used to being called Son by Gram. I was only twenty-three when your brother was born." He doesn't mention Jayme's being born.

Twenty-three seems old to Jayme. She knows some kids twenty-three who are divorced. One guy was remarried. Maybe Son can't be a father or anything except a son. "Arrested adolescent," Carver, her Human Relations/History teacher would say.

Jayme wonders what Carver would make of her family. Joe wants to be called Joe, because he is Joe. Not Gramps, or Papa, or Poppy.

Gram was highly unusual—Helen's expression—to let herself be called Gram, not Allison. Helen had added Baldwin to her name, paid a hundred dollars to a lawyer to add it. Now she is Helen Anne Baldwin Patterson Burch. Baldwin was a family name, an old one; she had traced Nathan Joseph Baldwin back to a land grant outside Wilmington, North Carolina.

"Everyone has a land grant," Son yelled, "somewhere. It's pretentious. They owned slaves."

"What do you think 'Brookwood' is?" Helen says back.

"But no slaves for us," he says under his breath.

25

Helen thinks the name Baldwin will help her in a way Jayme doesn't understand. "Well, pretend to understand," she says. "In the real estate business, when a client is asking her: "Oh, which Baldwin are you and then saying we're the New England Baldwins, New Hampshire Baldwins, the ones the Museum is named for." The new name will enhance her business of selling old Virginia properties to people who want homes that reflect a heritage, a lineage, something.

In class Carver had handed out faded Xeroxes that ran down the page about Oedipus, he called him Ed-i-pus; Gram said being Greek it was pronounced Eedipus. He killed her father, but by accident. So what's the big deal, Jayme wondered. You can't help accidents. There's no point in worrying about them; they are just out there waiting for it to happen. They are facts.

Jimmy drove into the oak tree for no reason, except he was tired or lit up on beer. Jayme didn't want to kill Son, even though Carver said everyone wanted to kill, more or less, his or her parent. Son had decked old Joe once when he was sobering up because he wouldn't admit he'd been drinking, and Jimmy had stopped Son from hitting Joe again. Old people do make you mad. Jayme knew that for sure. Jayme had taken Gram upstairs the night of the fight where they sat on the bed listening to Son and Joe yell. She can still hear Son's explosion, "You have!" and Joe's slurred dignity in, "Alright, you know so much."

Carver's Human Relations class was really a history and sex-education class. The Xerox paper on Oedipus was supposed to have something to do with sex but Jayme didn't see that either. A story went around school how Jimmy, right in the middle of a discussion of puberty and glands, had asked, dead serious, why Indians never had zits. It made you think. White kids envied the clear skin. Maybe that's a Hollywood version of indigenous people—happy in the virgin forests before syphilis came. Mainly they talked about herpes and AIDS, Trans people and how to think of the spectrum of sexuality or gender because they were current events. For her mini-term paper, Jayme had used two Time magazine articles on VD. She did it without Scott's resources.

Since Helen and Son's separation there is more sex in the air than before. Helen had found a used condom by her brick walk and accused Jimmy of being "crude and inconsiderate." She had been to a conference on selling yourself, not property, and "trusted Jimmy and Jayme to take care of themselves" while she was away. She insisted they come for weekends with her but usually she was "out with a client" or at a conference.

"It's not mine. I'm on the pill," Jimmy had grinned. "Ask baby sister. She's old-fashioned—virginal, against abortion."

"I wish," Jayme had said. Then she remembered how they used to pick Helen up and swing her, one, two, three, onto the bed. She wished they still did that.

"Has she gained a pound?" Jimmy had asked Jayme over Helen's screams and struggles.

"Up to 110, I think," Jayme said back. They knew Helen's fear of a pound or two settling in on her. She always ate standing up. "A theory of mine," she said. Another theory was never to wear a sweater or coat in the winter. "More calories are burning, you see, to keep you warm." She had one dress coat and a down vest she wore for looks. She was critical of looks and thought Neal "could be very attractive if he tried. Not that he had to try hard because he had gone to preppy Belmont."

"But Jayme's fifteen pounds too heavy. And she keeps her hair too long," Helen would say as if Jayme weren't there. "Today, all girls let their hair go long and lanky. It's a phase they're in."

"I could say the same thing back to you, but I won't," Jayme said.

"Go on, I'm through my phases and I'm tough."

"Sure." Jayme knows that her mother's views of hair and weight, phases, and of her as an also ran in all of the life races.

Jayme knew she was going to apply to the University where Neal had applied. The last time he'd seen her she was giving her last—she hoped—piano recital and had played "Moonlight Sonata." Even Helen had been impressed, not that she was there to hear her play.

Part of Jayme wanted to be one of the pretty girls her mom admired, not the girl with surprising talents—like playing "Moonlight Sonata." Not the girl who needed math tutoring, not the girl who played goalie for the soccer team. The distinction is important, she tells Scott who says they're all alike—girls in the pretty range. The not so pretty ones want to get on a ten-speed in OP shorts and a white Head shirt. It's not a vision; it's one she has heard Neal describe. That girl is Jayme's ideal now too though she knows it is out of date. She lists her perfections for her ideal girl in her head.

She's going to The University in the fall, the only one in her class who is going there. She's going to study sports medicine. The math will be a problem. She doesn't do dope, she told Neal the day they went to the four-wheel drive at the bodacious mud race deep in the woods.

"That's what college is for," he laughs. They both laugh because he has been smoking weed since he was twelve. Later he advises her, "Say 'computers' when people ask you what you want to do."

That day on their excursion to the mud race, Jayme killed a black snake crawling toward their blanket out of the woods. "Look at that sucker," she said, and then cut the snake so it lay in two neat parallel strips. She wiped her buck knife.

"You should be a vet," Neal told her. He had never been to a mud race.

"More money in athletes. They need every kind of therapy and surgery. More money, and therefore, more fun."

"You're older than you really are and you sound like your mom."

"I met your mom at the aerobics class when I substituted for the teacher. She seemed good to me. Determined. Perfectionist." Neal is saying again, "Look at that sucker. You did a good job on him."

"No, I mean look at the Blazer going for first place in the Mud Bog. The Bronco won last year, but I think the Blazer will go this year." Jayme yanks her hair back into a ponytail with both hands, says "Jeez" and lets it fall back in thick shining brown blades.

Son has a Blazer, a four-wheel drive, diesel and likes hearing any good news about it, since he has sent it back under warranty twice and it was recalled once—transmission and brakes. At supper Jayme will tell Son about the hundred-dollar prize the Blazer won, and he will be impressed that the fancy preppy kid Neal had gone and had liked it.

"Is that what you call good news?" Son asks Jayme.

"I thought it was," Jayme answers and starts upstairs to cut off Gram's light and cut on her fan.

"That you, Jimmy?" Gram calls out. Sometimes she says, "Who goes?" She says it's from Shakespeare and it's the only Shakespeare Jayme has ever heard out of school. Old Joe did say, "To pee or not to pee, that is the question," when he was drinking.

"No, it's me, Jayme," she answers.

CHAPTER 4

Jayme feels she is too young to have so much of a past or the present she lives with—divorced parents, dead brother, and alcoholic grandfather, grandmother who either has dementia or pretends she has it. She knows so many dead people and people almost dead. She had seen in the *Reader's Digest* a test for stress and she added up her score to an eight on the scale. Just being kin to Helen's family alone was a killer. Helen's father's divorce when Helen was Jayme's age was the old-fashioned bitter kind, not the no-faulter like hers and Son's. She seemed to enjoy telling Jayme, "I've been through worse. You should try going to court and testifying against your own father."

At times, Jayme thinks she would like to tell someone, maybe a judge, what a killer it was to have unhappy parents. They did not need adultery or domestic abuse to make them unhappy. Oh no, they had each other to do that, Jayme yells in her head.

She taps on one of Joe's Purple Martin bird houses with the tall pole Joe keeps just for that. Sometimes chipmunks run out the little porthole windows and down the pole, but once a hive of bees went crazy, disturbed and then organized themselves into a dive bomber before Son got the spray that dropped them in their attack. Son kept saying, "I hate to do it, but it's you or the birds."

It sounds like an old movie to Jayme when she thinks about Helen's life as a girl, what she had lived through and come out as Helen; adultery, country-club fights on the patio, thrown glasses—"Waterford," Helen adds when she tells the stories—lawyers and finally, the suicide in Scottsdale, Arizona, of Helen's mother. Within a year Granddad Baldwin had remarried—a rich widow. Who else, Jayme always thinks. So if Helen can "pull up her socks" as she always says, then Jayme certainly can who has no suicide, parents who have a friendly divorce, no adultery, no domestic abuse. Just a dead son. The favorite child.

Polly, the rich widow who for some unfathomable reason married Granddad Baldwin, has a birthmark splashed over one eye like a pony and puts purplish brown eyeshadow around her other eye to match. Jimmy used to try to guess which was which. Polly liked asking them questions that proved to their Granddad, what country hicks they were. "She thinks we're grits," Jimmy told Jayme, "and Son wishes we were more country than we are. He thinks we're city slickers."

"I don't know what we are," Jayme answered.

Once Polly asked them if they had ever heard of Plato. "Not Pluto, my dears."

Jimmy had shut Polly up on that one when he said, "Yeah, Plato was Socrates' best student, his word processor who wrote down every word his teacher said." Jayme didn't know Plato and Socrates knew each other, and she wondered how Jimmy knew. Being in college prep track must have been it and having Mr. George Washington Carver for his teacher as Jayme does now and has to put up with, along with everything else, being a disappointment to the teacher because she is not Jimmy. She knew Jimmy had taken all the extra "Enrichment" classes that were offered sometimes. "Can't hurt me," Jimmy had told Son.

"But what can you do with them? Can you make a living from knowing all that?" Son had asked.

"The classes are offered to make the teachers happier, and good grades in anything look good to college admissions and scholarship committees," Jimmy had said.

"I guess that's so," Son had said.

Jayme remembers Polly telling Granddad that Jimmy thought he was smart, then she added, "To be Helen's children, those two, the two J's, haven't been out that much." Helen almost died when Jayme had told her what Polly said about them because Helen prided herself on giving the Jimmy and Jayme "Opportunities." Some of these opportunities were summer art or music classes at the museum. Polly had divorced Helen's father after a year, an event Helen called "As inevitable as an earthquake."

Grandparents were divorcing more and more. Jayme heard about these all the time, but it would never happen for Joe and Gram. Joe says he's waiting for the Big Divorce, the Black Hole, the Big Beyond, the ride to the church to solve his problems. Gram would never leave Joe if she were offered the Parthenon, she has said many times.

Two years ago before they knew Joe had cancer, and the emphysema seemed like a health nut's idea of a disease, he had fallen for the family counselor Helen had dragged them to.

"It's all of us. We're all in it together. Family counseling helps everyone."

It did help Joe. He spruced up, went to the dentist and took Ms. Kent, "the interventionist," the plums and blackberries he had picked. Gram had watched him, packing the fruit carefully in Son's Eskimo cooler.

"What's a single girl, that Ms. Kent, going to do with all that fruit?"

"She's forty-two," Joe answered a question Gram had not asked.

"Half our age almost. There's nothing like an old fool," Gram said as they drove to the Center. Joe didn't answer but he had quit drinking during the six weeks of counseling, so no one cared if he made a fool of himself, sober, or not.

Jayme has decided divorce is good for everyone. It's the best thing for everyone unless it's your own parents. It's good for grandparents. But divorce for parents is really bad. Jayme often thinks of Son's and Helen's arms and legs instead of their whole bodies or selves. They danced, made babies, made her. Now they fight as often divorced as they did married, only over the phone or in messages garbled through Jayme's or Gram's or Joe's delivery. Their divorce is not working.

Last time the fight was over football practice. Helen was supposed to drive Jimmy to the mall to be picked up, but she couldn't drive him because she had to meet a client, so she sent her friend Paula. Son was furious that Helen could not be bothered to take her own son, "her only son," he added.

Ms. Kent had assigned them *When Bad Things Happen to Good People* to read and a book about the stages of grief. Joe said the title was stupid because when bad things happened to bad people, it was good. Besides, he added, he didn't know any good, really good, people. He read it though, because of Ms. Kent. Helen started it, but said it wasn't as good as the *Cinderella Couples*. It was funny—not ha ha funny—that Ms. Kent got them to read about grief and bad things <u>before</u> Jimmy drove into the oak tree. They had thought they were just another unhappy family. Now they feel unlucky as well.

Helen is angry at Joe again. "Again is a sad word in this family," Jayme says to her.

"Say what?" Helen looks madder.

"Again is sad for us because we repeat bad things."

"Well, I certainly hope you aren't going to drive into an oak tree."

Gram has told her many times that some thoughts lie too deep for tears. She said a poet had written it. But Helen's thoughts don't seem deep. She seems mad at Jimmy for dying and madder at Jayme for saying anything at all.

Helen is sure that she is the good person. The bad things that have happened to her all come from Son's family.

Jayme has pointed out that the Baldwins are no prize.

"Look at that Polly-person," she yells, "for example."

"She is not a Baldwin."

"Well, Granddad is not exactly a winner, is he?"

"Compared to many people, your Granddad Baldwin is a Grand Sweepstakes Winner!"

"How is that?" Jayme wants to know.

"He cares, we Baldwins care, for the finer things. He saw to it that we had tennis lessons, swimming lessons, he taught us how to ride. These are just some examples."

"What good did all those things do you?"

"Why, we met nice people." Helen saw the trap she was walking toward. "Your father could be a very nice person. He has it in him, but he didn't develop it."

Divorced, Helen insists on Gram's coming to her parties, even keg parties as if Gram were a college girl, as if Helen herself were, and finally, Jayme has to agree with Son here, that Helen thinks as if Gram were still her mother-in-law, as if there had been no divorce.

It's nice someone wants me to go somewhere," Gram says when Son insists Helen is using her to get to him.

"I'm so off base, most of the time, out in left field, that I don't see how she could recruit my help in any way," Gram says lucidly.

"Information is power, Gram," Jayme says, quoting the one thing she has learned in Communications Skills. "Mom loves to know what house Dad is wiring, whose stereo system is broken or if he has trimmed the boxwood. Why, I don't know."

"You just said why, Jayme," Son looks at Jayme, surprised at the allegiance to him instead of to Helen and her perception of her mother's ways. Son is used to thinking that no one knows Helen as he does. Jayme would like to add, "No one is supposed to know her as well," but he rests on the point he has made about her loving to know stuff.

Gram resorts to a cliché, "I'm still the grandmother of Helen's boys."

"Boy," Son and Jayme say together.

"You know what I mean," she says.

Son says, "You sound like your ex-daughter-in-law."

Jayme drinks milk straight from the gallon jug, pumping glugs out and down into her throat. The rim doesn't touch her lips and if she lifted the plastic bubble of milk higher, just a little, Joe swears she could go in the Guinness Book of World Records.

Jayme doesn't like to hear Joe and Gram try to be modern. Joe had told Ms. Kent that, and she had looked amused. Counselors should not be amused. It was hard enough to think of something to tell them.

Helen wears her denim skirt and cowboy shirt to go dancing at the Black Horse with her friends. Jayme thinks Gray Martin likes Helen and in the dark music of the Southern Outlaws playing, they look like a couple. Helen is "definitely not interested in 'tea and sympathy,'" her euphemism for sex. Jayme wishes she would use the word "relationship" or "privileges" like other people do to mean sex. What Helen definitely is interested in is money, and she is sure that contacts like Gray are the name of the money game.

Sitting in the booth at the Black Horse, the pitchers of beer beading in lines down to the coasters, Jayme is happy that they look like a beer commercial, except she's here with her <u>mother</u>. She is a child chaperoning her mother. Helen draws a happy face on one pitcher and turns it to face Gray. She seems so friendly. A lot of the kids there would probably like a mother like her but Jayme knows that she has come only to make contacts. She is filing away what she hears for tapping later into her list of Contacts. Helen says almost to herself, but Jayme has heard her, "Everything fits and anything helps." This is her motto on her memo pad. She is asking Gray about his grandmother's old home on the river. Jayme has heard Helen say it'd make a gorgeous country club.

"Let's dance, Helen," Gray pulls Helen out of the booth. Gray looks down. This is a golden oldie, "Bobbie McGee."

How much more embarrassing can it get than to have her mom dancing like crazy with Gray.

Jayme guesses that Helen gathers information at her aerobics class too. One of her Apple programs is called "Trailers" and when she punched RUN, she saw all their assessed values.

Son's family, the Andersons, did not offer Helen any contacts. Joe had been a house painter. His brothers were carpet installers. Gram's family were the "genteel poor" which meant they couldn't do much. One of them, though, had become a judge. But he had studied law, "read law" Gram said, in jail. He was there for shooting a preacher who looked at his wife during his sermon on adultery. Gram said there were standards then, moral standards of right and wrong.

It's not clear to Jayme what is the right and the wrong in the story of the judge and the preacher. And the wife. Why did the preacher look at her? Murdered for looking?

One thing that seems right is Gram's "contacts" with nature. Helen appreciates nature only at the beach or while skiing.

Son's three calves are an effort to make a contact with nature. Son has inherited this talent for connection, Jayme believes, from Gram. Silly or not, it's a better kind of contact than Helen's.

The next day Jayme takes Gram out to the "orchard," another miniature, doll-size enterprise of Son's. The four dwarf cherry trees from the Burpee catalog have just borne fruit for the first time, a pie's worth of cherries. Jayme admits they look as good as Food Lion's. She's glad Son will make the pie instead of Helen who would use condensed milk and graham cracker crumbs for a cherry goulash and call it a Cherry Delight. Son will put them in a frozen crust with sugar and butter, flip another crust over the top, prick it and bake it.

The June apples are ready too, though it's July. "A bad season," Son says glumly, as if he were a farmer from Iowa on "60 Minutes" who's telling his woes about his corn and the Federal Land Bank's foreclosing.

The mockingbirds are crying like babies or cats or sea gulls. Cats are the only things they could have heard to mock, Jayme thinks. The little trees throw big shadows on the grass she has just cut in circles around the trees. The wind is blowing. "How's that ocean breeze?" Jayme asks Gram, looking at her through the branches that are bending low with small green apples. Gram somehow picks five apples with each hand. It's Burpee's Harvest Plenty breed for people with small orchard plots. She hopes to tease Gram into laughing like Jimmy used to. Going out to the orchard may remind her of the real farm in Nelson County where she grew up. Peach and apple trees spread over the mountains. She remembers her great grandfather had shipped Queen Victoria ten bushels of the Albemarle Pippins every fall. She remembers the deep-dish apple pies, and the peach cobblers made with sweet biscuit dough.

Gram smiles but doesn't answer Jayme about the ocean breezes. She seems to be recalling mountain air and the orchards.

"Do you think it is at all possible for eternal life to be here in the sunshine on us, the shadows on your cut grass, the birds making a racket about us taking the apples from them?" she asks Jayme.

"Why not?" Jayme answers too sweetly and too quickly. She adds more sincerely, "It's OK by me. Makes sense. "She tries to talk the way the Born Agains do at school because she thinks Gram would like a fuller discussion of eternity. So she asks, "Could it be in the Honda's racket too, or Son's yelling at me about Algebra and threatening to keep me from going to the Spring Fling?"

"Why not?" Gram smiles so brightly at her that she feels like she is Jimmy for a moment. They fill a green plastic bucket with the green apples. Gram says, "One milk bucket full."

"It's a dog bucket, not a milk bucket, Gram. This is not a farm."

They walk across the grass to the ranch house. The green Masonite siding has been hosed down, the redwood trim has been oiled. It took Jayme two weeks of hot, resentful work to wash and polish the house. Other people had real work. They didn't run a one-woman nursing home or a Lincoln Logs Farmette.

Stepping into the chilled kitchen, she feels better about things. She gives Gram a peck and cuts the air-conditioner down. Gram calls it factory air.

"Catch you later," Jayme says.

"Right on, I gotcha," her Gram answers.

CHAPTER 5

Every year the August Spring Fling was held during Dog Days. A calf and three pigs were barbecued, a band played. This year The Outlaws were hitting the overcast heat hard with their music. Two days of hot fun.

Neal had on madras Bermudas and a pale yellow polo shirt, silk knee socks and penny loafers. Jayme had on almost the same thing—except she had no socks on with her loafers. "We are period pieces, museum quality," Neal smiled. He had come for the weekend.

"Should we get married?" she asks Neal.

"Later, Fool, later."

"Just checking it out."

They had been at the poolside party all day, had taken many dips, eaten plates of the barbecue, slaw, rolls and pie. The beer was kept iced in four old bathtubs with claw feet lined up by the patio.

"Do you know Gray Martin's family?" They own this old place. Jayme asks Neal who seems to know everything. He sees Della's son Ricky and waves who yells "Hey, Man," back.

"I know Ricky but Gray, just a little. He's got problems with his mother."

"Who doesn't? I am sure Ricky doesn't have any with his mom Della who helps us with Gram who loves her. We all do."

"Well, Gray's wants him to be a surgeon so he can afford to keep up this antique place. This is a real pool—concrete and Italian tiles, not a vinyl-lined one. It's a real house, too. 1758. Real rugs. The works. A solarium, if you know what one is."

"Of course, I do. What's the problem then? Gray's got the smarts, doesn't he?"

"Gray wants to farm. Ricky wants to play football and do physics. His path is straight and he and his mom see it the same way: scholarships."

"Should Gray be put in the state mental hospital? No one wants to farm now. In fact, farming should be outlawed."

"No, to really farm, big time. In modern way. There are at least a thousand acres here and he wants to go to The University and study farming, so he can do it right, organically and somehow make money."

"I think he's an idiot," Jayme says, thinking of Son's pulling the tassels off his six rows of garden corn to cross-pollinate them and making cucumber barrels at midnight.

"Son worries himself crazy over seven acres. What would Gray do with a thousand, plus this pile of bricks to deal with?"

"Jefferson, Thomas, designed it. It is your basic mansion."

"Big deal."

"Don't knock it, 'til you've tried being rich or living like the rich."

"How do you know so much?"

"My rich uncle in Lauderdale."

"That's different. Florida's rich is tacky."

"Money's money."

"Well, this has the style, as Scott would say, of a family that didn't eat itself up like most do."

"Scott wouldn't know style in the road."

"Yeah, he does. He's chosen her china and silver for his bride, poor girl."

"He told me he copied your Mom's patterns not Gray's mom's."

"Is he queer?"

"Ask Janette."

"You sound like Scott."

"Thanks a mil and shut up. Here comes the man himself."

Scott was loping down the terraces to the pool. He was prep today too in khaki and pale blue. Only a touch of plaid in his belt. Sockless. The earring gave the only true note of her criminal personality and it was almost hidden in his longer than usual hair so he looked like a college-bound student.

"Come my man and maiden fair. We're off to the Smash, the demolition derby. The Pontiac and Fairlane are parked nose to nose in a gully Lady Astor-Martin wants filled in. We got to bust them flat, do her a favor and when sweet little Gray is a brain surgeon, we can come for martinis on the terrace and gaze at the landfill we accomplished in one evening's play. So, drink up, me hearties, me buckaroos. This mayhem and destruction are permitted, free and legal destruction, our Vietnam, our 9-11, our Iraq, and the Middle East. Ukraine. Deadass.

"Let's go then, you and me. And see what we can see." Jayme takes Neal's cool un-calloused hand. Her hands are tougher. She works in a nursery and has been rooting azaleas and boxwoods all summer. Her fingers are like cool new pencils. They walk half a mile into the woods. The band is starting up above the deep gully.

Sometimes she wonders if Neal's good manners, "impeccable" Helen would say, are automatic. Son reacted to Helen's manners by hiding his own. He was honest he said and distrusted mannered people. It was true that manners were phony, but they gave you room and some privacy, Neal had said when he talked to her about it. He thought they held civilization together.

They watch Scott pick his way down into the ravine. The cars are fitted in the long ditch so tightly, the doors can't open so he slides in through the window like the stars of "Nazca." The Pontiac is dark green, almost black, and against the dry red dirt walls of the small canyon with the honeysuckle growing in swirls along the edge, it looks like he is entering a new underground life where people have built shelters after the nuclear war. The cars are set nose to nose, hood to hood, facing each other. The Ford had been dragged there by a wrecker and dropped in. The Pontiac had been driven in.

"How come you could drive it? Thought it was a junk car," Jayme asks Scott.

"Man, when you say drive, you mean highway, cruising, stopping, gassing up, regular driving. This Old Lady, a beauty, is from 1936, a luxury after the Great Depression, when people needed some beauty and style in their lives. I got it because it needs work that only a very skilled mechanic could do. It was designed by a genius so Google says, one Harley Earl, who had a head for money too, rose to the top at General Motors."

"Where'd you find the band?"

"Does the word cacophony mean anything to you, you, Baby?"

"Yeah, I've seen it on vocabulary tests, and don't call me Baby."

Neal says, "It means chaotic noise and that's what you have here. What time do people come? I will have to leave early."

"At nine, just at dark. I've got the weapons laid out over there. I suggest the splitting maul but maybe the crowbar is more feminine."

Jayme gets a sledge hammer and Neal says he'll sit this one out, then leave. Kids are gathering. Some in swimming suits with tee shirts, some in jeans with no shirts. Scott yells above the music. "I want twelve men. Maybe a girl or two. All white breads. A long boo goes up from the crowd. "Six men or boys, okay, one or two girls, whatever, per car. Timed destruction. Musical accompaniment. No injuries allowed, I mean no complaints about smashed toes, glass splinters, or hacked knee caps, just hub caps."

Scott is standing on top of the pale blue Ford delivering the rules like a valedictorian. He had cut on his radio and found the oldie station-- Emmy Lou Harris is knocking out a song. He ends his speech by saying he won't be a team member. No, he is the judge. Flatness of each car is the standard they are to set for themselves. He divides them into teams, the Imps and the Frigs. Jayme is made captain of the Imps because the four boys on that team are from out of town.

"That's not much of a reason, not much of a confidence vote," she yells at Scott.

"Shut up. Pretty Girl. This is your first time. What do you know. Enjoy!"

Scott is telling the other team, all local yokels, to let the drunkest team member do the windows. "They don't feel the flying glass and aren't as babyish about blood."

"If he's counting on me to give out tips like that, he's crazy," Jayme thinks.

"Come on, shake hands, teams." The teams are standing on the cars, axes and tire irons by their sides. The crowd of about twenty is up the hill. The Southern Outlaws are waiting for Scott's signal "Ahh one, and two…" He gives it. The music bursts open the twilight and some birds fly up from the underbrush. The first hits are tentative taps. Then the Ford's windshield shatters. The teams start dancing and whacking the cars good naturedly. A slam dance festival. They pound in rhythms careful of each other. One fellow slips off the Ford into the tangle of vines behind it and is helped back up. There are cries of "Watch out," and "I'm going to get this one."

Jayme's bush axe has a half-moon blade and cuts into the Pontiac's roof and hood. It's hard finding a moment to raise her arms and come down with a karate yell with the four strangers pounding all around her. She sees blood on the rumpled roof and tries to yell to Scott who is walking up and down the rim of the gully with a stopwatch and drinking his usual Heineken. Bud is for rubes. The music seems to be drawn into the ditch by the sledging and beating. Jayme's shoe is wet inside and she thinks her foot is cut, but it doesn't hurt. The other Imps have cuts; she knows she nicked one on the thigh. He can't stand on the car now. They are leaning and lying on it. The Ford looks flatter than the Pontiac whose radio is still going but Jayme can't hear what song is playing. She sees the light above the station buttons. She wants to smash the radio and feels it must be the last sign of life in the old thing.

Let the air out of the tires," she orders her team.

"Stupid, just slash them," someone yells to the Black kid who is fumbling with the air cap. He stands up looking angry and lets someone else sink his axe into the tire, then does all four in four strokes—looks like an expert. He's got a funny haircut and someone said he was from Philly.

"Time!" yells Scott. The Outlaws stop with a drum roll. The teams scramble up the banks. They look like they should be taken to the Emergency Room but their girlfriends and Neal rush up with cold beer. They seem to be sucked away into the darkness. Jayme can't tell the Imps and Frigs from the other party-ers. Neal says they should go home. Ricky is nowhere to be seen. There's nothing to say about all this. Nothing polite. She needs time to tell Scott what an idiot he is. She feels sick and certain that her dreams about Neal have crashed and feels her foot bleeding.

Scott is measuring the cars, walking over them like a cat. At the highest point, he stops, pulls out his silver measuring tape that springs back, and measures. The Ford is three feet, nine inches. The Pontiac is four feet and some. There's no one left to listen to Scott's closing remarks. The band is packing up and laughing about something else. Scott wants a ride home in Son's Blazer which Jayme had driven for the first time this summer.

"Why not?" she says to Scott.

"Too much for Neal? Did he have to go home? Curfew? Homework?"

"Probly so. Guess so. But it shows how much smarter he is than us."

"Don't be ridiculous. You know you feel better. I heard you yelling down there and beating that old Pontiac, to death."

"It was a car, not a person, not an old woman," Jayme says fiercely to Scott.

"Same difference," Scott says before Jayme slams on the brakes and leans over to open Scott's door to shove him out.

"It's only ten miles home. Use your contacts to get a ride."

"No problem. Stay cool, Little Sister. We have more in common than you know. I saw it tonight. Did I upset you, Precious?"

Scott is lighting a joint and standing in the moonlight grinning. "Go home and get some rest. You're going to need it, my Girl. The next step is sex, the real, not the teen stuff you and your Preppy do."

CHAPTER 6

The digital clock on her radio said 1:20 when Jayme stared at it. It was the last time she looked before she fell into a violent sleep. The next morning her bed looked like there had been a dog fight in it, knotted sheets and smeared blood. Her foot was purple and the gash on the top had dirt in it. It was 11:40 when she woke up the first time. Her muscles were burning, her head was going kaboom over her left eye. She could hear soft scrapes and off-center hits from the kitchen.

"I missed your first two pills, Gram, did you get them by yourself," she yelled from her room. Sick, she thought, Sick, Sick, Sicko. All of this.

"Yes, indeed, Jimmy," Gram called back confidently and cheerfully.

"Great."

"Joe's gone to town."

That meant to the liquor store and for almost the first time, Jayme envied Joe his insulation from the world, especially from personalities, responsibilities, and the word came to her— consequences. What had Scott meant last night when he'd said she would need some rest? Probably just an expression. The sinister sound was typical of Scott. Where had Neal gone? Disappeared. Gone. Couldn't take those country pleasures?

Gram was calling something. Jayme grabbed for a pair of jeans and started into the kitchen. She could hardly put her foot down, her clutch foot, for the riding lawnmower she still owed for. Son had been gone for hours. Jayme knew she should go to Dr. Thompkins and get a tetanus shot before Son saw her foot. At least, he could say she'd used her head and gone to the doctor.

"George Stewart has been here this morning."

"What for?"

"He has something for you but didn't say what it was."

George Stewart was the sheriff who saw his office as part of God's plan for running things.

"He's coming back at one o'clock."

"Why didn't you wake me up?"

"I don't know. Something told me not to."

Jayme checks Gram's pill bottle and sees that two are gone. She's on schedule without her help.

In the shower, Jayme tries standing on the bad foot. Blood oozes and then runs down the drain. She washes it, hoping the dirt had made it uglier than it really was. When she steps out on the red mat she thinks maybe she is lucky. The blood is running onto the rug but once there, it sinks into the red fuzzy fibers. She hops to the towel cabinet and finds the red towel to wrap her foot in. She is lucky not to drip blood and have to clean it up.

By one o'clock, her foot is dry. She has taped the cut shut and poured Apinol on it. This is Gram's favorite medicine that she buys for her at the hardware store. It smells like pine tar and probably kills, she says, even the thought of a germ.

The two-toned brown sheriff's car glides up to Brookwood. Stewart gets out with an "Awful sorry, but this is the way it is" look and comes to the door. Jayme has washed her sheets through two cycles, flipped the mattress, remade the bed and except for holding one foot slightly off the ground, she looks okay. She hasn't had time to call Neal and doesn't want to anyway, doesn't want to know anything about when he left the party, the madness.

"I'm sorry, awful sorry, but here's a warrant for you. Court is set for next week. Judge Macon wants to settle it before school opens. You read it."

Jayme reads slowly, not able to understand the drift of the formal phrases. Slowly and then more quickly she gets the picture. George W. Carver, the teacher at Central High School, was swearing out a warrant for Josephine James (Jayme) Anderson's arrest on the charges of and stealing an automobile, a 1936 green Pontiac. The only name on the warrant is Jayme's.

"You better get a lawyer, Honey," Stewart says.

"I don't know any."

"My nephew's one. Don't know if he could take you, but people say he knows his stuff. He's in the book under G. M. Stewart, same as me, only he has Atty. After him."

He gently and slowly twirls his hat. "I'd better be going. Give my best to your Grandmama, Mrs. Anderson."

Jayme tries to prioritize" as Helen says. Should she go to the doctor first or the lawyer, or find Son and go directly to Mr. Carver and explain things? Call Neal? Or kill Scott?

Only killing Scott would help her. Now she understands the local team and the strange team. Jayme had been the only local beating up and wrecking the Pontiac. Now she understands, in a way, why Scott said she'd need some rest. She decides to call Scott.

His answering machine says that Scott has left for an extended vacation across the country. Jayme had laughed at Scott when he had gotten the answering machine. Now that makes sense too. She calls again. Same answer.

Dr. Thompkins doesn't ask any questions. He talks to her foot. "Looks like cutting wood got you in trouble." After getting some free samples of Darvon for pain, Jayme leaves. Wouldn't Scott have loved to get his paws on these pill-freebies?

Now to call Neal. His voice is as cool as beer. "I'm not totally shocked. By any means," he tells her when he's heard the story. He thinks Scott was probably bored and set up the whole thing. Scott stole the car from the one teacher Jayme got along with, admired, never criticized. Scott chose the teams for the smashing, got it going, then left. It's the perfect teenage crime in a way. Jealousy, revenge without the trouble of a gun: cars, music, beer, partying.

Neal understands more than she has understood about Scott. It's not a good feeling to be one who has been stupid and another person has gotten it.

"But Scott couldn't be jealous of me. Jimmy maybe, but not me. And Scott likes my mom. He would not want to jeopardize his standing with Helen. He wouldn't ruin her chances with the Martins for making a real estate deal. She wants to make a country club out of the place."

"Don't kid yourself. He was tired of you getting all the sympathy for having a dead brother, a helpless grandmother, well almost helpless, a drunk grandfather, and a classy mother. He hated you for having such a family. Even dead, Jimmy is better than no brother. Drunk, Joe is still your smart granddad, even senile, Gram is your sweetheart Gram." And to top off the list or why Scott targeted her, he added that Helen had danced with Gray and seemed to like him. Leaving Scott out in the cold.

"Another thing," Neal goes on, "they'll never find Scott. He's gone. This was his school boy phase. Now he's beginning his adult life of crime, I just know it."

Neal is getting upset. His voice is beginning to shake, something she hates about herself when her voice breaks down. But it marks how serious he is. Jayme is in real deep shit. As if she did not know it. Still, any sympathy is very good even if it freezes her heart and brain because it is on the money. That word makes her know her life is over. They say goodbye.

George M. Stewart, Atty., says Jayme must throw herself on the mercy of the court. The Pontiac was almost a collector's car—an antique—because of its fins and restored interior. Just the chrome alone would cost a fortune to replace. Sheriff Stewart assumes Scott is out of the picture and in fact, doesn't think he has much to do with the case. Her attitude is "Well, boys are boys and this boy may have been worse than usual, but we must deal with what we have. One guilty person, You, Jayme Anderson, whose foot is injured, 'self-inflicted' he keeps saying, and one stolen demolished car. Witnesses all over. Cut and dried. Pay up and shut up."

Sheriff Stewart's son, the Atty., thinks the judge will assign Jayme work in the community to pay off the car. What is Jayme good at, he asks.

"Old people."

"You're kidding me. Can't stand them myself. I know I shouldn't say it to you, bad example and so forth, but I always say, when it's time to go, go. This hanging on and ruining everyone's life is for the birds. I've got my folks in Ivy Manor. They're happy. They don't know what's happening. They don't know me anymore, anyway."

"But you know them," Jayme says looking at the degrees framed and hanging behind the lawyer's desk.

"Oh, I'm grateful and all for what they did for me to get me through school. But my life is my life, you see, and I've got to live it. It will help you with the judge to like old folks though."

"I saw your new boat when you pulled it by the cemetery."

"Yes, I'm having *Carpe Diem* painted on it. Nobody will know what it means, but I had to take a Latin course in law school. All the terms, you know. I bet you don't know what it means, Jayme."

"Something about grabbing all the gusto you can, I think."

Jayme feels sick from not eating and her foot is throbbing. Far worse is her certainty that she herself, she alone is to blame for this disaster. On impulse, she decides to stop by the Carvers on the way home. She does not know if she will survive it. She will pass out.

It's a log cabin set back in the pine trees, no grass to cut, and a split rail fence around the lot. Jayme guesses it's about an acre there. A blonde pony runs up and down the fence the way dogs do in a pen. The cabin is neat, the yard swept and there are ruffled gingham curtains at every window. There are decorations in the yard and along the front porch. A propped-up wagon wheel with wooden spokes, and old horse-drawn plow is the mailbox, and an iron bell hangs between two posts at the front steps.

"Do I pull the leather thing?" Jayme asks herself trying to focus on the unimportant and let the tsunami hit her in a few minutes. Lift the cabin, the Carvers and her up into the sky.

"Pull the rope," Carver says coming out on the porch. He has on a shirt that sort of matches the curtains, Wranglers and boots. He looks different from the man in the classroom in his poly-blend pants and shirts that don't fit. Here he looks okay, a real person, even if his home reminds Jayme of a set for "The Little House on the Prairie." His wife comes out of the dark slit that was the front door into the sunlight. She looks like a country-western star in tight jeans and the same blue checked shirt as her husband's and as if she is coming onto the stage.

"Barbara, this is Jayme Anderson. You know, the one who wrecked your Pontiac." Jayme feels like she is about to lift off out of the yard, Wonder Woman style, her head is so light. She is spinning above the Carvers and herself.

"That's what I've come to talk to you about."

"Well, talk is cheap. Go on."

"I didn't know it was yours."

"So?"

"I had been told it was a junk car from Gardner's junk yard."

"Who told you such a thing, first? And when you've answered that one, tell us, didn't you look at the car?"

"Scott told me, and I guess I didn't look."

"Everyone knows Scott is one step away from the state penitentiary. You shouldn't have believed anything he said." Carver is keeping his Marlboro Man cool. Barbara is sitting on the porch railing swinging her leg and tapping her fingers on the railing.

"That car was Barbara's baby. She had restored it for the rally this October. We're talking big bucks."

At Jimmy's funeral Jayme didn't feel this terrible. Now she feels worse—feeling so desolate over a car and entirely responsible for ruining it. She hopes she will have to have a wheelchair. For Jimmy's accident, she was innocent. But now, she is guilty and in hell. Carver is going on.

"You could say, in fact, I do say, you killed our baby."

They turn away, and go back into the house. Jayme stumbles back to Son's Blazer. If it were really hers she could give it to them to replace the Pontiac but they probably wouldn't take it. She can hear them exclaiming in horror, "What, trade babies!" And at home, Gram's and Son's "What, you gave away the Blazer!"

Now there's Son to face. It's four o'clock. He won't be home until six. Jayme decides to go home, get Della to leave, wash Gram's hair, and talk to Joe and cook supper.

CHAPTER 7

By six, Jayme has had the ribs going for an hour. She has a bucket of deli slaw in the refrigerator and the quick-rolls rising near the oven. It's a supper designed to please Son, and will to some small degree, if he eats it before he hears the bad news. If only Gram doesn't start talking about Sheriff Stewart's visit. If Joe isn't too drunk to eat.

Another minor danger is that the supper may set off the memory in Son of real meals. Real bread, real slaw hand chopped, ribs basted in real homemade sauces. Sometimes Son goes a little crazy over the fake food they eat, though he's one of the best "phony baloney" cooks in the world, he says, every time he makes a pizza or a box cake or opens a can of Chili-O.

Gram's hair shines across the table. Jayme got her to put on her pink alligator shirt and she looks like an angel. Her new glasses are halfway down her nose. Joe looks like a turtle, sleepily, drunkenly sticking his head in from the porch to ask if Son is home yet. He's gauging his drinks. He can belt one down just as Son walks in the house and he won't look as drunk as he actually is. In fact, he has a theory, he tells Jayme, that one stiff drink sobers you up for a while before it takes effect.

They hear the Blazer roll up. They hear Son's holster of equipment slapping his legs as he comes in. They try to read his mood. He seems to sink down in his clothes after he sees them.

"Can you blame him?" Jayme asks herself, "but wait until after we eat and he hears the news about me. He'll be six feet under."

Son looks at Joe on the porch, and doesn't bother to shrug. It's not worth a shrug. He looks at Gram. "Where you going, Gram, all spiffed up? Out to the Black Horse with the young people?"

"A good looking young man turned up today and took my eye."

"Where'd he take it?" Joe tries to come in from the porch with a joke. His bourbon has prepared him for some fun, but it has also slammed the family gate in his face. They prefer him sober; he prefers to be lit.

They all, out of habit, stare at Joe as if he were a new breed of lizard. Jayme pulls her lizard image back in, and grins at the red rib on her plate.

"Here's a good one," Jayme is desperate to get them through supper. "Why aren't Polacks pharmacists?"

They look up at her, giving their full attention to the question. They are surprised and a little pleased that she is politically incorrect or culturally incorrect. They don't want anything bad or hard to handle to happen.

"Why?" they ask silently.

"It's hard to get those little bottles in a typewriter. I mean it's hard for <u>Polacks</u> to get the plastic bottles in so they can type the prescription. This is a way out-of-date joke because now they print off the labels for the little bottles from the computer. Jayme knows she would be killing the joke by explaining it. She knows she is being cruelly inappropriate. In fact, her hero is a Pole, Jan Karski, who reported about his visit to the Nazi death camps in 1943 to FDR, who could not believe it until later. Mr. Carson had told her class about this great man, and now she had ruined his car, his child.

"Pretty good," Son says. He looks surprised at Jayme's joke-telling ability. Jayme's supper, Gram's shining hair, Joe safe another day—all go by uncommented on, but the Polack joke is appreciated for what it is, xenophobic as Neal would say, dated as Helen would say, not that funny everyone else would say. So it's good that only the hard core group at the supper table heard it.

"What young man, Gram?" Son asks again, staring at his plate looking like he might enjoy his food for the first time since Jimmy's wreck and some conversation, even some gossip.

"The Stewart boy was here," Gram says. A smear of Hickory Hearth sauce is on her chin. Son wipes it off reaching across the table.

"The Sheriff, that one?"

"I guess. He had a big car and hat. I saw him out of Joe's window."

"That's what I've got to tell you, Son. The sheriff brought me a warrant. For wrecking a car at the Martins' last night." Jayme feels light headed and sick, like she might fly straight up through the green roof of Brookwood.

"Whose car were you driving?"

"I wasn't. We wrecked it with sledge hammers and axes. Scott told me they were junkers."

"Scott? Cars?" Son is sinking down in his chair.

"Yeah. A Ford, a piece of junk, and a Pontiac, which belonged to, only we didn't know it, to one of my teachers, Mr. Carver. His wife's too.

"You're telling me this story mighty easy and calm. As if you might not go to jail."

"I've been to a lawyer and to see the Carvers."

"And?"

"The lawyer thinks the judge will sentence me to do community service in a nursing home, because of Gram and Joe. I'd have to work enough to pay off the car."

"How much is that?"

"Mr. Carver said the book price not the antique or the collectors' value."

At this, Son walks angrily over to the sink. With his back to them, he fills an iced tea glass with water and drinks it. It always has seemed to Jayme as if he were putting out a fire in his stomach. She remembers Jimmy telling her about a Spartan who for some reason held a wolf under his shirt and let him eat his stomach until he fell dead. The point was, Jimmy said, not to let anyone know your problems until they killed you. Not even then. Jayme had asked Jimmy what about Helen and all her faith in family counseling. "For the birds," he had said.

Son drinks another glass thirstily. Joe shakes his head as if to say what a waste, such a capacity for drinking. Son looks at them this time and runs a third glass and brings it to the table, shoves his plate away and sits down heavily.

"It's time for Gram's pill." Jayme is not avoiding "confrontation" as Helen calls fights, even if it looks as if she is doing exactly that. She divides the day up into medicine times. Every four hours, Gram takes a captopril tablet cut into quarters. Usually after the 7:30 pill, Gram gets ready for bed with Jayme handing the gown with her eyes shut to give Gram some privacy.

She always says, "I'm not looking at you. I've got my eyes shut." As soon as she says this, Gram limbers up and struggles with her gown.

Tonight, she doesn't know what to do. The usual routine won't work. But Gram has to get out of the pink shirt. It'll be a skin-the-cat time because it has only three buttons.

Son looks at Jayme and says, "I'll wait to talk until you and Gram are squared away."

It takes an age to get up to Gram's room, the only room with a real antique, a walnut dresser with a mirror in grays and silvers. Ever since her English teacher, that Ms. Hooper had made them learn a weird poem "Pied Beauty," Jayme sees beauty in streaks and "stipples." The mirror is stippled like the trout in the poem. She turns on the lamp. More flashes and shadows on the ceiling. The mirror is tilted to make a full-length reflection. She and Gram look like two characters from books: Pip, the boy, and Miss Haversham, the old witch. Only Gram is too soft and mush-minded to be witchy. She can't leave her, she thinks, to struggle out of the shirt and into her gown. She might fall and break her hip as the doctor says she will sooner or later.

There's no point in worrying or thinking about Son. He'll take over the conversation and tell Jayme what she should think, what will happen, where she went wrong and why she is always wrong. He means she is not Jimmy and never will be.

Dead people are more powerful than they get credit for being. Maybe shrinks and Family Counselors know this but most Americans don't. What would Jimmy have done? He'd have been on the Ford's smashing team. He would have done the legal thing, but still had the same amount of fun—so-called fun. I'm the stupid nerd.

Jayme's foot feels hot and tender, just as it had through Gram's shampoo and supper. "Time for my pain pill, I guess," she thinks but doesn't take any. "I better save it for after Son finishes with me."

At last, too soon, Gram is in bed, flashlight ready, water ready, Porta-Toilet ready. "Don't let the bed bugs bite," Jayme whispers into Gram's silver feathers of hair.

"You too, my sweet."

Son is washing dishes, a job he never does. He is carefully washing the glasses first in water that is steaming up through a layer of bubbles. The dirty dishes have been organized into order of their greasiness. The rib bones are in the compost bucket. Jayme picks it up to take out to dump in the compost hole.

"Wait on that. Tell me again what happened."

"I helped beat Carver's Pontiac, not into scrap metal, but damaged pretty good because Scott had gotten the smash thing together. I thought, like we all thought, that Mrs. Martin wanted the gully filled in with two smashed junk cars. Scott had us organized in teams—the Ford smashers were working on real junk, but my team, the people from somewhere else, I don't know where, were smashing the stolen car, it turns out, the Pontiac. Only it was Mr. Carver's antique prize car. Now Scott has gone off somewhere and the other kids have too. I'm the only one anyone knows who's left around here, so I got the warrant."

"When is the hearing?"

"Next week."

"What charges?"

"Larceny and assault."

"On a car?" Son seems to be thinking along sympathetic lines but it's too early to tell.

"What lawyer did you go to?"

"The sheriff's nephew."

"Why did you do a fool thing like that?"

"I thought I'd better do something."

"I think you better go to Weldon Turner."

"Suits me. The lawyer the sheriff suggested, his nephew, his parents in the nursing home.

"I am not surprised."

Son has shown more interest tonight in what she has to say than he has for a long time. He is scrubbing the broiler pan that Jayme had cooked the ribs in and she is drying the dishes. They have a very efficient system. Usually Jayme and Gram do the dishes, and it takes hours because Jayme has to redo the washing or drying.

"We better go to Turner in the morning. I can see you might owe for the car since you were idiotic enough to smash it up, but I can't see why you should have criminal charges on your record for the rest of your life."

The sink looks better than it has for a year. Son is scrubbing the stainless steel with a Brillo pad and squirting it with the scalding water. They can see their faces looking down into it.

Jayme can see herself next to Son. Their eyes are set back in their heads. Until now, she has always felt she looked like Helen's side and Jimmy like Son's. She forgets and puts her weight on her bad foot and grabs the sink, surprised at the spurt of heat and pain shooting up her leg.

"Something else. I cut my foot when I was wrecking the car. Dr. Thompkins gave me something to take and wrapped it up."

"Let me see."

Son unwinds the dressing and looks at the zippered gash. There are pink streaks splaying out from it.

"Did he give you a shot?"

"No."

"You should have gone to the new clinic. Dr. Thompkins can't see as well as he used to."

"I thought I'd better do something about it."

"Right. That's what you said about the lawyer. We better run over there now."

"You sure?"

"Sure I'm sure. I'm sick of arguing with you. If you want gangrene we can stay home and watch TV and let it fester."

Jayme is happy to hear the familiar tones of sarcasm and fury, happier to hear them in the if-question: "if you want gangrene" instead of in the direct attack: "You went to the wrong lawyer and doctor." She decides to use Jimmy's strategy: friendly fire.

"You're the one holding things up, Son. You're keeping me waiting. Waiting for you to polish the sink is enough time for the gangrene crud to take my whole leg off."

It works. Feeling better, Jayme hops to the door catching hold of Son's arm to get down the back steps.

"I like these flowers. What did you say they are?"

"Hollyhocks. Their leaves cure gangrene."

"Sure, sure they do. Tell me another one."

CHAPTER 8

The phone rings. Jayme knows it's Helen who wants to know the whole story: the dollar amount of damages, what the sheriff said. Jayme won't mention her injured foot, but then she does. She has been to the Martins already and then to the Carvers. She feels she has done what she should in these terrible circumstances that she is responsible for. She hears herself want to ask her mother a childish question. No one held a gun to her head and made her attack the 1936 Pontiac, the prized possession of her favorite teacher. Still, her sympathies for herself run high, bringing tears to her eyes.

"Where are your priorities, Helen? I'm here, my injured foot propped up memorizing the 'Barefoot Boy, one of Gram's favorite poems.' I could use some TLC," Jayme tells Helen in her head and then says the words into her phone to the beat of her throbbing foot.

Helen as always can hear Jayme's thoughts, but these are words. "You don't deserve any sympathy. I know you'll be all right, but how could you have been so dumb, plain <u>dirt dumb</u> to listen to Scott? If he said it was raining, I'd plan a picnic."

"You seemed to like him at Christmas. And dancing to the music. Him admiring your china and everything."

"At Christmas, I would have liked Frankenstein. I think Scott is his long lost son. Maybe Eva Braun was pregnant and escaped from the bunker or so I've read. Maybe Scott is that baby."

"Where'd you read that crock?"

"Some legit historian."

"Come on."

"Listen to us arguing about Hitler. I want to know what the sheriff and lawyer had to say."

"He said tell the truth and volunteer to pay for the car alone. By myself."

"That doesn't sound like good advice to me."

"Son and I thought it was."

"I see."

"Don't you want to know how my foot is?"

"Yes, of course I do." Helen sounds preoccupied.

"Pretty good. And don't you want to know what Mrs. Martin had to say about the violence on her land?"

"Of course I do."

"She said she had often thought of turning the place—it's called 'Brightley'—into a country club."

"I meant, I want to know what Mrs. Martin said about wrecking the cars and the trouble." Jayme is getting the familiar porous feeling she gets from talking to Helen. She is so angry, her brain swells up, but she makes herself answer.

"Oh, she said that she thought filling in that ravine would be one of the first steps in making a golf course. She said Scott had come to her after Christmas and asked how he could help her. She told him she'd been widowed two years and she appreciated his offer especially because it was so practicable for the rough of the course. She said practicable, the right word, of course."

"How's her little baby boy, Mr. Perfect? Gray? Did she say?"

"He's fine. She told me she has set up a trust fund which becomes his the minute he has M.D. behind her name."

"What would our friendly Family Shrink, Ms. Kent, say to that way of raising a kid? Wouldn't she say you shouldn't have to bribe kids into being successful? Scott would love to take money for any reason from anyone, And especially take it away from Gray who does not want to be a doctor any way. His heart is set on farming Brightley's thousand acres."

"Beats me. I'm through with my dreams about that property. I'm turning in another direction. Now I'm a little interested in EST."

"Mom, that stuff is as old as Elvis or Chuck Berry."

"I know them both—"Heartbreak Hotel" and 'Blueberry Hill.'"

"Nope, Wrong again. That was Fats."

"OK, OK. Get off my case."

"Don't worry."

"More later." Jayme rests her foot by watching old, dumb "Tic Tac Dough" on TV and eating chocolate and banana pudding pops together. One bite from her left hand, one from the right. She is trying not to think. The charges against her may be reduced. Son is hoping they will be reduced to Disturbing the Peace, but since "Brightley" was a thousand-acre place, originally part of a land grant from King George before the Revolution, it doesn't seem likely to Jayme that Judge Macon would go for criticizing the Martins in any way.

When Jayme thinks about Scott, her foot goes crazy with pain.

"Hope springs eternal in the human breast, Man never is but always to be blest." Gram is saying this as she putters around. Whenever she gets to "Never is," Joe sings out, "Preach on, Sister." The real meaning, Gram has explained to Jayme, is hidden in the words "to be." Jayme hopes she will be able to use it in one of her summer book reports. It might be tricky working it into a review of *Washington: Man or Monument*. She had too much pride to do *Animal Farm* again this year, but it sounded like the quotation could be worked into the first paragraph.

Neal answers the phone in his vacation voice she calls it. During school he usually has a scholarship voice. He wants to be a Rhodes, Wilson, or at the very least, a Danforth Fellow. College will be like high school for him after Belmont Preparatory—a necessary evil, then real life will begin.

"How come you like me? You're so smart." Jayme really wants to know.

"Hey, that sounds like a good song title. Maybe your talents are in song writing. Have you thought of that?"

"Not recently. I've been fighting amputation threats, consulting with my lawyer, having stressed-out phone calls with my so-called mother, and dosing up my paternal grandmother. The only duty I've neglected is going to the liquor store for my grandfather, and I would do that, if my wooden leg had come from the factory."

"Prosthesis."

"Say what?"

"You say wooden leg. I say prosthesis."

"You say prophylactic. I say Trojan." Jayme thinks she's gone too far this for a girl who allows no privileges. There's a long pause. "I'm sorry," she mutters.

"You're cool, it's good."

"Not exactly."

"Look on the bright side. You've still got two legs. Your dad is helping you. Scott has gone away, probably forever. You'll be a senior, and last but not least, I'm talking to you."

"Actually, now that you've explained it all to me, I do feel some better, You PWK (Privileged White Kid)."

"Good. Now, I also have an attractive option for you. I have arranged, at my own expense, a trip of the kind I might enjoy—not to a demolition/criminal event, called in Southern Speak, a Derby—but to the Dell to see *The Mikado*. Light, bright and sparkle aplenty. You pack a supper and I'll pick you up next Thursday at six. You may come to be a superficially cultured person with whom I can be seen occasionally. It will take your mind off wrecking other people's prize possessions. That's one of the values of culture. It alleviates guilt for what we have done. Hitler loved opera and stole paintings."

"Thank you, Mr. Minister of Culture. You'll be sorry one day to have condescended to me when I am running the United Nations."

"Yes, yes, my Sweet Girl. I love you because you think you are funny. See ya and love ya." He presses her shoulders up close to him and leaves.

Jayme hopes he does love her a little. She does love him a little. He does make her feel better, much better, actually. Is that what love is, feeling better?

Things are improving slightly. She gets up and hops through the house to the kitchen where Gram is trying to fold the towels. "Allow me, Madam." She folds them the way Helen does when company's coming. She remembers she didn't tell Helen about her talk with the Carvers. She takes out her phone and hears Helen's very friendly, personalized answering voice. She wants her mom to call her back today.

Helen gets back to her to report that the Carvers were very nice but adamant. She could see their point. Their pride and joy was stolen and then damaged for no reason. They were sorry Jayme was a victim of Scott's viciousness, but it was more the principle of the matter than anything else. Property should be respected. They could not, on principle, Helen repeated, drop the charges. They would not object at all to Jayme's being sentenced to working on a civic or community project to pay off the car. Maybe the Rosenwald school in the county. The Carvers were upset that the law made no allowance for the Pontiac's being collectable. It wasn't old enough by five years. If it had been, they could not have afforded it and besides, Pontiacs weren't made then. Their insurance didn't cover vandalism, which canceled out the theft clause. It's a catch-22, Helen said at the end. She perfectly understood the Carvers' points, and she thought Jayme did.

"I do. What can I say? The fact is I helped ruin the car without checking out what Scott said. It gets me, though, how those other boys are free as birds and the other team that busted the Ford flat are free too. No one else got hurt even. My foot feels like it had some bones removed."

"Do I detect a note of self-pity?"

"You got it. That's right. Have a good day." Jayme hangs up. She yells at Gram, "Is it pill time?" even though she knows Gram wouldn't know or pretend she doesn't. A few minutes couldn't hurt her to wait. Jayme needs a few more minutes on the poem Son had laid on her to memorize that morning. This sucker is longer than "If" by a long shot. What would it feel like to be Neal and learn anything she looked at? He probably has a photographic mind, the iPhone of his school. I have a Kodak Polaroid brain that spits out too early, and then the picture is gray and slick with brain juice.

When Jayme finishes learning a stanza of "The Barefoot Boy" she limps out looking for Gram who's watering her rhubarb plants. She can tell she forgot her pill and that her "blood is high" as Della says. Her face is red and Jayme can see the vessels flickering at her temples.

"Here's your pill, Gram. Come on in. You need it now."

"I'm coming, Jimmy."

"He's the other one. This's the Jayme-girl." Joe says from his in his chair in the shade. He is smoking and burying his cigarettes as soon as he finishes.

Jayme flops down. She doesn't know if Joe knows anything about the car. She sticks her foot up as a conversation piece, but Joe takes pride in ignoring it. His rule for social life is that if someone wants to tell you something, she will. Just wait for it. Never question.

Dutifully Jayme begins and feels Jimmy inside her head phrasing the story for her. The dead do live on. At times.

"No time like now for crime."

"What did you say?"

"I said your buddy Scott did me in. Now the law is on my tail."

"Scott's not my friend. He's yours. There's nothing to that boy. Anybody could have told you that." Joe is practically lecturing.

"Whatever. He rooked me into smashing up a car night before last at the Martins. Turns out it was my teacher's car."

"What's he teach?"

"Human Relations. History. Social Studies. Whatever."

"What's all that? The only one I've heard of is History. Not to know it means you repeat it. Looks like you tried to repeat your brother's wreck."

"Wrong. That never crossed my mind. I wish it had."

"Who needs to go to school for those things?"

"I do."

Joe has heard enough. He turns the yellow cat over with his slipper and rubs him with his soft leather toe until the cat is asleep. It's late afternoon and the heat is making it hard for Joe to breathe. His shoulders move up and down but his face is like a rock.

Gram walks in front of them, trying to water the yard, pulling the hose from off its spool by the faucet.

"I know you're thirsty," she says to her English boxwood and rhubarb plants as big as lawn chairs. She fumbles with the nozzle and drips some water on the cat. "I'm sorry, Buttercup."

"You got my foot, too," says Joe.

"Did I?" She turns the nozzle on full blast and cuts it over and down on the pink trimmed rhubarb stalks.

"Look what I'm doing, Jimmy," she calls. "Could you come help me, please?"

"I'm here," Jayme answers.

CHAPTER 9

Liberty Manor Nursing Home is not a bad place. Jayme has been working there three weeks. The judge ordered her to carry her check to the Carvers every two weeks and endorse it over to them. This personal delivery of payments would, the judge hoped, "impress on her and all young people the importance of respecting property in and of itself. Nothing should be destroyed. To do it 'in fun' was wanton and criminal. The extenuating circumstances, he said, softened her sentence to some degree--to work at Liberty Manor instead of going to the reformatory at Lorton.

Lifting the patients out of bed into wheelchairs and bathtubs is good for Jayme's muscles. There is a very strong and trained young Black man to show her how. Amir is pre-med and going to the University. She likes the way he is so sure of himself, never showing that he is tired. He likes working on the schedule of times for meds, baths and bed. At home, her responsibility for Gram and Joe is vague and endless. Here at Liberty Manor, everything is specific and timed: baths, haircuts, bed changes, meals, visitors, music. And there is the excellent Amir to do things right and on time, and good naturedly.

Neal has come by once. He is impressed by Jayme's newly acquired professional ease with the elderly men and women. She bathes the women who are too far gone to do it for themselves, but who still hold on to remnants of their younger selves, their modesty, and Jayme honors this.

"Mentally-wise, they're beyond modesty, but they have muscle memory about their private parts," Jayme explains.

Are you afraid it will turn you against your own womanhoodness or old women like your Gram?

To answer him, Jayme bats her eyes at him like an old time movie star, knowing that Neal will hope that she means more than she means about any use of her own private parts.

The Olds have their pied-beauties. "The freckles and moles on their skin are actually a turn-on, kind of…mentally-wise, I mean. Their wrinkles tell or suggest interesting, okay, sad stories."

"Do you ever think of your own future older, golden years?" Neal laughs.

"It'd be hard to avoid, living with Gram and Joe. I can see that my DNA will drag me into going the same way with cholesterol, carbs, and booze. What I can't imagine is being forty-three or so. Those middle years seem a desert or a wilderness. Looking at Son, I can't say enough depressing things about being in the forties, although Son has solidly helped me this summer. You know one of the biggest helps Son's given me is not being surprised at my own criminal nature, or how it is possible to be a danger to others and to myself. I am still shocked about Scott. I want to murder Scott and if I ever find him, I will put my hands around his throat. First I'm going to rip out that earring. But back to Son. He's always, quote, back-at-the-ranch, unquote. Brookwood must be the only seven-acre plantation-ranch-farmette in the Sunbelt. I see him staring out at our ranchero 'into the sunset.' I wish he would talk more to me, but what's there to say? I can see why he can't live with Helen. I can't. And I can see how he drives her around the bend. Son can't stand her friends. The "Drinks on the Terrace" crowd. Scott and Sheriff Stewart are the only two who have been to the house since Jimmy wrecked. Helen is more of a teenager than I am. She acts my age better than I can with all her cool friends and with-it clothes."

"Give it the old college try."

"I've decided I am not going to college."

"And how shall I introduce you? My wife, the person who couldn't leave home? The failure, the drop-out who never started?"

"First, you can be a failure, a dropout <u>with</u> a degree. Second, are we getting married?" Jayme wants to jump toward Neal more to scare him, but her foot still hurts when she puts her full weight on it. His face lights up thinking Jayme wants to kiss him, but to be on the safe side, he gags after sticking his finger down his throat.

"You can be a more interesting failure or dropout <u>with</u> a degree. Failure is titillating. Remember what I told you I learned without meaning to learn anything from Miss Gifford's class—" Success is Counted Sweetest by Those Who Ne'er Succeed.' She said it when she handed back tests. She tapped me on the head with my test.

"I never understood why the word never is shortened to <u>ne'er</u> in poems. It should be <u>nev'r</u>. Why is the <u>v</u> left out?"

"See, Jayme, you do have the mind of a scholar. That's the kind of stuff they think about. Stuff like the word never spelled right ne'er helped anyone."

"P'raps, my dear. But back to my fascinating family."

"Do go on."

"Let me sharpen the old hatchet up for Helen. She always claimed that Son worshipped Jimmy and loved me. And that of the two, love was better."

"Isn't it, Herr Dr. Freud?"

"Well, eet iss und eet ain't. Vorship geeves a boy zee room to grow and at zee same time to be admired." Jayme pulls at an invisible goatee.

"What does love do, poor ole love, then?" Neal laughs.

"Love is too close. I guess you could say, it's too human. Love coming from irregular people is irregular. You have to deal with it as is, all bent and screwed up."

"I didn't know you were so deep." Neal is drinking a Coke in his Yeti cup as they sit in the Lounge for Visitors at Liberty Manor. It's Jayme's break, fifteen minutes. The Coke comes out in beads down the sides between sips. The more he sips, the more it foams up and down the sides of the cup, down his elbow. Neal leans over as if to kiss her, and then whispers "Coke is it. This is a love scene. I wanted to bring you a Bud, but I was afraid they'd catch you and send you to the Big House. That might not be a bad idea. You could go to college for free, convert to Christianity or Islam, be rehabilitated."

"Can't I be all those here in an old folks' home?"

"Hope springs, you know what. And I could have the coolest bride, a jailbird."

Mr. Wright wheels by the lounge, catches sight of Jayme's brown legs, arms and hair, and yells out her one greeting, "How about it?" He keeps wheeling, yelling to the ancient crones dropped like handkerchiefs in the long recreational hall. A church group is singing around the piano down at one end. The hymns have been arranged into hillbilly love laments. "Jesus, Lover of my Soooul Comfoooooort meeee."

Dr. Thompkins is part owner of Liberty Manor. He wants two patients per room and refuses any Medicaid or poor patients. Jayme wonders where they go. Maybe they stay home and some teenager like her takes care of them. Dr. Thompkins refuses long-termers too. He wants turnover.

Jayme goes into room 302 where Mr. Johns and Mr. Parker are—both are full-pay singles but were put in a double. No one minded or complained. They are recovering—a joke with the staff—from hip replacements. Mr. Johns wants to talk, Mr. Parker never says a word. Even when his children come, he looks at them and then turns his head. His meds keeps him sedated but not enough to addict him, in case of an autopsy after he dies. Mr. Johns' children never come.

Jayme's shift is the graveyard one, 11–7, so she deals with the sleep walkers and the dying. The night nurse, Mrs. Gold, doesn't want her to call her until the patient is "out." Then she takes over with the futile formalities of efforts to bring the person back to life. She makes the phone calls and does the paper work. Jayme covers the patient with a sheet and rolls him out, trying to lie to the roommate. "Just running Mr. Smith down the hall for an IV check."

Dead people are stored in a chilled room with a garage door for easy pickup by funeral home drivers.

When Jayme gets home at 7:30 AM, she's starved but has a hard time eating. Sometimes Son's breakfasts of ham in red-eye gravy, grits, scrambled eggs and truck driver coffee help. They look so healthy, so hearty, she can't resist them after the night at Liberty Manor. Gram isn't up because she gets up at three in the morning and by seven is asleep again.

Joe has lived three or four short days and nights by morning. In a way, Jayme has more privacy at home now that she works than she did before. Because she works at night, Joe and Gram respect her sleeping. They don't feel free to call her, even though they forget at times. Della doesn't call on her either. About three times every week, Jayme has to work a double shift because the morning orderly doesn't show. When she comes home at three in the afternoon, she's dragging and Gram and Joe have forgotten she's been at work all the time. They do better when she works just one shift. They don't understand why Jayme goes to bed at four o'clock in the afternoon, just as Gram's rerun of "The Waltons" comes on.

Jayme wonders how she will manage school and Liberty Manor. She's up to 121 pounds on the Liberty Manor diet of creamed chipped beef and candied yams. Judge Macon anticipating her hardship had said, "It's your little problem, Jayme. I worked in a cannery all night when I was coming up. Didn't know what a shift was. We worked all night, every night. Then we went to school and worked at home. Boys don't sleep. Boys work. And now, the same goes for girls. My wife reminds me that women have always been on duty 24-

7." The Judge's son is in Jayme's class but looks forty years old. No one knows him much, Jayme suspects, because he is working two or three jobs. Coach Turpin wants Jayme to run patterns and lift weights now for track. How will she run and work at Liberty Manor?

It will be next October when the Pontiac is paid for. Judge Macon settled on $13,206, half the blue book price, and all of it must come from Jayme. He thought the Carvers deserved at the very least that. Jayme agreed and still does, plus she is grateful. The Judge said that Mr. Carver had told him that Jayme was a very good student like her brother Jimmy had been, and had been friends with the Black students, not being offended but smiling at her nicknames, Becky, White Stuff. She had helped the class have good discussions of Critical Race Theory, giving a report on her own coming to understand the ways that the systems that seemed invisible can be damaging. He knew her family had suffered a great deal from the death of Jimmy, but to have been in on the damage to the 1936 Pontiac whose Boxwood Green original paint was what he and his wife were especially proud of was beyond what he could believe. It was a terrible blow at first not just when he saw the doors and the fenders crumpled, but later when he tried to understand that Jayme had not stopped the vandalism or even as far as he knew, tried to stop it. He had seen her turn the tide of anger in their classroom, one time even jumping up on her desk and yelling, "Hold it." She had restored order and calm. He felt for her because he had heard her called White Bread and Whitey and other racist names. Mr. Carver had gone on and on, Judge Macon said about Jayme's dream of going to medical school. Her term paper had been on the doctor who had come up with the One Drop of Black Blood that condemned people to being subject to racist policies and laws. She had included the Pocahontas Exception which according to this nutcase doctor gave Native Americans/Indigenous People an escape hatch from racist dangers. Her report had been a highlight for the course. Mr. Carver was dead set against all levels of racism and would often say that if he had been alive in Southhampton County when Nat Turner went on his killing spree of Whites, he George W. Carver would have joined in, but now he said, he knew that was not the way to change things. Ancestry.Com had shown him his own One Drop and he knew that truth and kindness were the only cures and might tip the scales of justice. So, he refused to ask for or allow more than a token payment, less than half the value of the car.

Helen is at the beach, Nags Head, in a condo with a woman friend. She used to say "girlfriend" last year, but after going to some support group, she speaks of her women friends. She had wanted Jayme to come for the weekend and invited Neal too, but Della didn't come to Brookwood on the weekends, and although Son was doing more and more in the house for Gram and Joe, Jayme couldn't imagine Son bathing Gram. If I can't go away for a weekend, Jayme thinks, how can I go to college, if I get my grades up this year? Maybe I'll take Gram and Joe with me. It's good that now I don't even want to go and Neal says I can go to prison and college there and then we can get married, if I will say yes.

Son giving Gram a bath? His mother? Never.

Gram is slick as a tube of shampoo in the shower. Jayme has worked out a system. She unzips and unbuttons everything. She gets Gram out of her clothes and into the shower to sit on a stool Son has bolted down through the fiberglass. Then Jayme gets the water temperature right on her stuck-in arm. Then full blast, and points it at Gram as she scrubs and swishes. "That's enough," Gram will call and then Jayme hands her a beach towel and she holds it more or less and is helped out, wrapped up and patted dry. She gets into her clothes, sometimes backwards but into them. She reminds Gram of some lotion. "Want a squirt?"

"Not much." Son couldn't do all this or he thinks he couldn't.

"So I do it," Jayme says to herself.

Joe, Son could bathe him, his father. Maybe. It was just an occasional bath for one thing—just before his chemo trips to the doctor, and they weren't regular trips.

Son has started driving Joe in for the treatment. That used to be Jayme's job. Son's also cutting the grass at the cemetery and golf course when Jayme works double shifts at Liberty Manor and can't get in her two hours of cutting before dark. He asks Jayme if Neal would like to come for pizza next week.

On the phone Jayme tells Neal, "Son and I are getting so palsy-walsy, so buddy-buddy, it's hard to deal with. He wants to know if you want to come eat pizza here. It's a big compliment to you to be asked to the halls of Brookwood. You'll be given the tour of the orchard, the north forty, low grounds and compost hole. The whole seven-acre spread."

"Sounds good. Your dowry that I will pre-enjoy. What time? Did you know my folks were in school with Helen and Son?"

"I bet they have some good stories to tell."

"Not to me, they don't. They just say how smart Son was, but that he never knew he was. He caught on to solid geometry and trig better than anyone."

"Why didn't he go to college then?"

"Too much in love, I guess. You know Helen's dad sent her off to a boarding school her senior year to get her away from Son, but he just waited until summer when she came home and they got married the day she came home. They must have arranged it all in letters."

"I can't imagine Son writing letters, especially to Helen. Or her to him."

"Then I guess Jimmy came along. Then you."

"Spoiled their fun."

"I guess so. I think I was the first fun my mom and dad had. Some people like babies, I mean some parents improve with all the trouble and expense of babies. Some are broken down by babies."

"Why don't you be a shrink, or at the least, a family counselor like that Ms. Kent who did a job on us," Jayme asks Neal, not meaning to sound sarcastic but knowing that what she's saying is mean. Neal doesn't take it that way. His good nature or his good manners at work.

"I just might. I like to think of you taking care of Gram and Joe. You'll be a good mom."

"How can you tell I'll be good? You know I'm a virgin, saving myself, not necessarily for you or not exclusively either-- all of me for the one I love."

"Who is the lucky guy? I hope it's a guy. I hope it's me, but maybe a girl would be better. Anyway, girls are not supposed to save themselves today."

"I hope you and I will though."

"Maybe, I'll try if you're sweet to me. Maybe not, if you're not. I'll invite you up to the first big weekend this fall. You can drive the Yukon, bring a cooler of Coors, or Buds, wear a preppy ensemble and take me...to the concert. Alabama will be there. Oldies are always good.

"Thenk yew, but until then, let's toddle along here with our golden years peers. Get tough for pizza night. You're the first real person here since Jimmy wrecked."

"Bye bye."

CHAPTER 10

When Jayme gets home from work the morning of the pizza party at Brookwood, the crows are going crazy and sound like broken computers. Their mild reasonable sing-songs have turned into random excited rasps.

Son is working the garden that never has had a weed and torments the hungry crows because he has white nets over the butterbeans and poled green beans. The tomatoes, "Big Boys," are growing in wire cylinders so you just reach in and pull one off. They're almost ripe. Yesterday Son fixed fried green tomatoes; thick green slices rolled in flour, salt and pepper and slipped into hot bacon grease. Easy as pie, he said, but when Jayme tried it later, wanting a whole plate full for herself, the tomatoes burned and stuck to the pan.

The crook-neck yellow squash vines are as big as the kitchen table and the blossoms are folding up into squash; some have a little tail of flower petals hanging out. The army of corn, eight rows, is over six feet. Son has rigged electric flashers that go off at night and whistle blasts during the day to keep the crows scared away. The beets have come and gone, so have the English peas.

Jayme knows she's the healthiest person going.

"I eat so many veggies in the summer, I can get through the winter on junk," she says to the circling crows.

Looking past Son in the garden, Jayme sees the three calves who are nestled down in the Kentucky bluegrass asleep in the sun. Butterflies, big black and blue ones, skip over the calves looking for manure and clover blossoms.

"Maybe this is all right," Jayme thinks and goes into the quiet house that still smells good from Son's breakfast.

Gram and Joe, one upstairs and one down, are sleeping. Joe probably got up in the night to read for a couple of hours standing at the kitchen table. Just this month he has read books on black holes, the Brooklyn Bridge and Alaska.

"I wish I had some interests," Jayme says as she picks up a book on Diamond Jim Brady on the table. Jayme gets a bag of books from the library every two weeks for Joe. She knows by now what Joe reads--any book of facts. But that's not exactly true either. Last year he got into weird stuff, Veilokovsky and Edgar Casey. After he'd read all that Jayme could find, he dismissed space visits and collisions as well as reincarnation. What Joe hates the worst is novels. Which is what Gram loves, especially historical romances or novels with rabbits and moles instead of people. Jayme has started getting all of Gram's books from the big print shelves. She reads the same books over and over.

The phone is ringing. Rickie, Della's son, asks to speak to his Mama. When Jayme says she hasn't gotten there yet, Rickie, thinking out loud, wonders if she stopped for gas and his cigarettes. "Tell her I'll be by about lunch time to pick up my stuff."

Jayme writes a note for Della. Gram worries about Della's doing so much for Rickie who is twenty-one and a guard at the state prison. "You'd think he'd be brave," Gram says and then tells the snake story. It seems Rickie Dale heard someone upstairs in the house where he and Della live. Rickie Dale's wife took off a year ago to go to Raleigh with the two babies, Rickie Jr. and Angela. Both of the babies need doctors, Gram always adds. The boy has a cleft palate and the little girl at twenty-six months has never walked. So when Rickie heard someone knocking over lamps, he calls out, "Mama, Mama." Gram imitates Rickie, "Get up, Mama, someone's walking around upstairs." With Della and her pistol, Rickie braved the dark upstairs and found a nine-foot black snake. He shot five times, Della right beside him. Then she carried the snake out in a box and buried him; she said snakes had wives or husbands or friends who would come looking for the lost one, so you had to be careful to always bury a dead snake.

"Won't they look for Mr. or Mrs. Snake even if he or she is buried?" Gram says she asked Della. "Yes indeed, but when they can't find no one they leave, pronto."

Jayme wants to eat and shower before Della gets to Brookwood. She eats the eggs and bacon and the fried green tomatoes, not burned, Son had left on the warm burner for her, drinks a big glass of OJ and hustles herself into the shower. Her showers are so fast and easy compared to Gram's. She dips her shoulders, left, right, into the hot spray, then her head, holds up her arms and that's it. Her foot is healing and looks like a monster's foot—purple and wrinkled. She hurries into clean clothes and goes to bed trying not to feel so wide awake.

Mr. Parker died last night at Liberty Manor. Jayme had thought he was just having a hard night with his breathing, so she sat with him and held his hand even though she wasn't sure old man Parker would like it if he opened her eyes and saw her. He talked, too, which he never had done. When Jayme said, "Want a drink of water," he had said yes, so Jayme held him up and helped him drink. The water mostly went down his neck, but some did moisten the lips, smooth and pale as the Styrofoam cup he was trying to drink from. Then Mr. Parker had coughed up a little blood, turned his head, and died. Mrs. Gold said, "Good luck," when Jayme asked her about calling the family. She took over then, and wheeled Mr. Parker to what they called the waiting room.

Brookwood looks bright and green instead of silly. Maybe it just seems beautiful after last night with Mr. Parker. The blue grass is soft and dark. Son lets it grow longer than the cemetery or golf course grass because it hurts blue grass to be cut close. When you walk on it, you leave your tracks. The day lilies stand in clumps around the mailbox and gate posts holding their pale orange heads up as if they are waiting for important calls.

Son is resting for a minute on his lawn mower. Jayme hopes he hasn't forgotten he is having a pizza party tonight. But if she calls out to remind him, she knows she'll say it wrong and make him mad. Better put on the lip lock.

When she wakes up at four o'clock, she hears "The Waltons" coming on. "That damn stupid family," Joe calls the Waltons. Della has gone, counting on Jayme to take over.

She's probably off buying Rickie a set of speakers for his Chevy Blazer, Jayme thinks. Then she remembers Gram is going to pay for her power boosters for the stereo.

Gram is tucked up under a blanket like one of her mole or rabbit book friends. Her dress is buttoned, only one button off, halfway down. Her glasses hang down across her mouth, fogged up. "You're a pretty sight, old girl," Jayme says to her. "Ready for your bath and beauty treatment?"

"Ready as I'll ever be," Gram answers without opening her eyes. She jokes sometimes when she feels bad, confused, out of her time zone, she calls it. The next time they go to cut grass at the cemetery, they should give her a ride. She jokes about dying like that.

Jayme gets the things ready for the bath. Three towels, one a big beach, Keri lotion for her shoulder blades, Estee dusting powder, Youth Dew for her arms and hands, Dr. Ammon for her feet, Arid spray.

After Gram's bath, Jayme tries to figure out how to ask Son about the pizza party. It's almost six. Nothing's been done. If he starts the dough to get it rising, he's sure to do it wrong; Son can make pizza crust and biscuits without getting gunk and goo on his hands or dropping any flour on the floor. Gram always says Son should have been a surgeon, with his hands. He can take splinters out of fingers with her pocket knife so easily you can't feel it.

Jayme goes out and sings, she hopes casually, "Pizza Hut, Pizza to go."

Son looks at her with his rattlesnake look. That is what Joe calls it, and he should know since he has the original unblinking "You have two seconds to live" look. But Son starts walking to the house, careful not to walk the same way through the tender blue grass. Jayme forgets and makes a bruised path across the yard.

"I see you're really helping tonight," Son begins as he washes his hands up to his elbows like a doctor.

"What do you want me to do?" Jayme is determined not to fight this one night. She'd rather have the "frozen north" night, Gram's words for Son's and Joe's bitter silences.

"What do I want you to do?" Son is outraged. Jayme realizes too late that the right thing to have said would have been, "I've washed the lettuce and made the salad dressing and iced tea." She tries to start the evening over.

"I'm getting ready to make the tea and wash the lettuce."

"If you looked in the refrigerator, you could see I've done that. The dough is ready to put down—which you could have done."

There's nowhere to go to get away from the bad scene. Gram and Joe will make it worse and Neal's being there is impossible to imagine. Not saying anything, Jayme sets the table. Son is always on her to do what's to be done without asking or talking about it. She thinks he does the same with Gram, but Son wants her to do everything carefully not asking or mentioning it.

Neal's brown Camaro shines under the Silver Beech tree. How did he drive up so quietly?

"Good luck to you," Jayme says to the ice she's clunking into the glasses. Gram has walked Neal back to the glassed-in porch where they will eat. Neal looks at Jayme, shakes hands with Son and helps Gram sit down. Without being asked to, she goes to get Joe and walks him to the table from his chair by the rhubarb.

"Rhubarb! I can't believe it. My grandma makes a strawberry-rhubarb pie that is wonderful. I didn't know it could grow around here. It always seemed so exotic to me."

"Lord, honey, you should see what we do grow here," Gram says. "Son will show you garden after supper."

Son says pleasantly, "I should have fixed a real dinner from the garden, but I thought all you kids ate was pizza."

"Come on, you're the original pizza man," Jayme says before she can stop herself and is shocked to hear Son's mild, "That's true. I love the stuff. But you'll have to come one night and I'll bet you a hundred dollars, the only things from the store on the table will be the salt and pepper."

"Don't bet with him," Jayme says to Neal. This seems to please Son too. It's a miracle.

Walking in the nine o'clock semi-dark, Jayme says, is one of the pleasures of Brookwood. She doesn't say why tonight, but she and Jimmy used to say that darkness hid the fact that it was a postage-stamp ranch. In the semi-dark, it could be South Fork or Tara—well, the ranch house would need to sprout columns and verandas.

The swishing leaves sound like rain; the vistas were designed by Son to trick the eye—in art history she'd learned some term for it that was on the exam for ten extra points. Jayme had gotten it right but now has forgotten it. She wished she could remember everything like Joe did. Joe could recite "Marmion," at least what seemed like the whole thing. Looking down through the grape arbor, you saw the orchard and a glimpse of the pasture beyond.

Another surprise or miracle in the semi-dark was Son's announcement that he'd made a freezer of homemade ice cream. Banana-peach. "Fresh peach, store bought fruit," he said. He explained to Neal how he made the custard; sixteen eggs, two gallons of milk, a pound of sugar, stirred on low heat until it thickened. Stirred with a wooden spoon. Add the fruit last. They hadn't had ice cream since before Jimmy's wreck. Jimmy had always turned the handle. Tonight Son put the freezer at Jayme's feet and started pouring in the ice and rock salt.

"I've never had homemade ice cream," Neal is saying.

"High time," Gram says clearly. "Bless your heart," she adds as the soup bowls fill us with the rich ice cream. It's the best Jayme can remember and she is glad that Gram has forgotten that she had told her that the old saying is condescending which Gram had said she could see how it could be taken that way. Like "You poor little thing."

The frozen lumps of banana and peach resist melting a second longer than the cream. Gram asks Neal to go with her to shut the chicken house door. She has six Rhode Island Reds. Son walks with them and turns them in the direction of the pasture. He calls the calves, Silky, Harriet, and Sawbones. They come to the fence, and he gives Neal apples to feed them. Jayme doesn't expect to get an apple from Son, but she does.

"Such a night, such a night. This is a night I cannot believe," Jayme tells Neal later when she is walking him to the Camaro.

"It was great," he says again.

"You don't know, you couldn't possibly know how different Son was tonight. He's in there now helping Gram get ready for bed. He never has before because it drives him crazy. Half hour to brush her teeth, half hour to get her blouse off, ditto for her skirt. It's not that bad, and I always exaggerate, but it feels that long, and he can't stand slowness. Joe's opinion is that Son is a perfectionist and anything less than perfect makes him crazy. Anyway, you brought out the best. I had dreaded tonight in a way, but now it may become my happiest 'teenage moment'. Well, 'night. Sleep tight."

"You may have some happier ones before you leave your teens." Neal is smiling up though the Camaro's chrome-framed window.

"Promises, promises." Jayme sighs and puts on her dog face the way Jimmy used to and break everyone up.

"Abyssinia Samoa. Call me." Neal starts the engine and backs slowly out of the drive lined with white pines.

CHAPTER 11

It is like summer except for the color of the leaves. Son's Lombardy Poplars look like yellow spurts of cookie dough behind the shed. The Maple by the gate was, Joe said, "firecracker red." It did look explosive. It was hot all day until night, then Son would say "Next week, I guess we'll have to build a fire."

Son's cast iron stove that he'd made for the den will soon be burning short logs. You load it once a day and the whole house is warm, not just around your ankles like it is from the baseboard electric heaters. But it is a matter of pride for him to start the first fire.

Neal is away at the university. His two letters have been long and friendly, but Jayme tells herself they don't seem like letters from someone she has told that he is engaged to be married. He has called her twice. He writes stories about his professors and friends. Jayme knows her letters are clunky—Helen's word—and probably begin with a topic sentence about the advantages and disadvantages of being a senior, taking Mrs. Rodger's English, Gilliam's Government and playing second string for Coach Turpin.

Neal hasn't mentioned her coming up to see him. She wonders if he remembers she had to work at Liberty Manor until she finishes paying off the Carvers.

What's wrong with a simple question? Something like, when can I drive up to see you? Jayme asks Gram as they slam through the dishes, not breaking any. Son redoes them most of the time, pointing out the greasy swipes on the plates which are plain when he holds them slanted under the fluorescent light. Gram can't see the grease and Jayme doesn't have heart, patience or guts to try to make her stop. Doing dishes is part of the spirit of a home, Gram says, and she is going to do them.

Joe looks at her like she's someone he doesn't know, but is still familiar with her crazy ways. He calls them to listen to something from the newspaper.

Clothes have been found in the landfill in the next county. The only ID was a silver knife in a pocket with the initials J.L.A. engraved on it. Joe stands up at the table reading.

"Didn't we give Jimmy a knife like that?" he asks.

Jayme remembers exactly. On her twelfth birthday he'd gotten her the thin, beautiful silver knife that had little scissors, blades, and a screwdriver that clicked into place, flat as a quarter. Jayme had wanted a knife like that so bad she could feel it in her pocket. Jimmy wanted her to use it and even take it to school on some days. At the wreck the night Jimmy died, Jayme had asked the rescue squad to look in Jimmy's pocket for her knife which she'd let him keep until he took the SAT's. It would bring him good luck not that he needed it. Yeah, right, some luck.

So she asked the rescue squad to look again in Jimmy's pockets. They had and George Stewart had brought the news "No silver knife" to her the next day. She felt she could see it, as beautiful as it was on her birthday when she had opened her brother's gift. Things, many of them, do not show what they have been through. Her knife out in Colorado would not show any signs of what it had been through. A little like the arrowheads and Civil War bullets Son found and brought in to put in the coffee table with glass top.

Jayme walks into her room. She knows before she looks that the knife is not in the dresser. She knows it went missing when Jimmy wrecked. Somehow. But how? She goes back and reads the newspaper report about the clothes found in the county landfill. They had blood stains and were described as khaki trousers, a blue shirt, 15-33 with a Brooks Brothers label. A turquoise earring is mentioned, but no knife.

Jayme is sure Scott has rigged his disappearance and now is in Boulder, attending a few classes without paying tuition. She knows he has her knife. She thinks Scott's is in Boulder because she remembered Scott's thing about skiing and Colorado. University of Colorado. U.C., Scott would say, was richer, better, fun-ner than any schools in the east or on the wrong side of the Mississippi. At the time, Jayme thought Scott was wigged out, whacko, on a rocky mountain high. Now she is beginning to think that Scott had set up the perfect crime. A prelude to the Spring Fling. Her silver knife he stole as a trophy. It's too much to hope that someone has really killed Scott.

Twenty years from now, Jayme imagines Scott's planned re-entrance into her life, laughing about the Spring Fling, asking how long Gram and Joe had been "gone" and offering some sympathy card words. He'd probably want to know how much the Pontiac had cost her. Jayme is furious.

The newspaper says there's not enough evidence for an investigation and offers Sheriff Stewart's opinions that the clothes were "typical of the uniform young people wear. Could be anyone's. Ordinary sizes. But the blood stains are not human."

Jayme mutters, "Vampire blood," as she stares at the sheriff in the picture at the site of the "non-crime."

"No body, no crime," the sheriff says in the caption.

Jayme answers the sheriff's picture, "Just so I never see that body again." She knows it's Scott's scheme of his own faked murder; the earring, the blood stains, the Brooks Brothers shirt, but her knife she'd given back to Jimmy, lent to him for the SAT's is out in Colorado in Scott's pocket. She will have to stop thinking of the knife. This was Scott's last message that he was smarter than all of them. He had stolen Jayme's knife from Jimmy's pocket.

Helen calls to say Scott must have stolen Jimmy's knife. She knows the clothes are Scott's too. "We think alike," Jayme says.

"Great minds…" Helen says and swipes Jayme off.

It rushes over Jayme that in spite of knowing what she knows that she is happy in a new kind of way. Doing what she can, no matter how small it is—helping when she helps Gram with her bath, finding her pills, checking out *That Was Trucking* and all the books on the Johnstown flood she can find for Joe. It is more real than some teens' lives, at least. And Brookwood, the funny little farm, is more a home, an effort at a home, with all Son's silences, than the homes that had sent their old people away to places like Liberty Manor.

One more call tonight. She punches in Neal's number. It's almost ten o'clock. The house is quiet. Son is asleep and Gram is just settling down. Joe will be up reading in an hour or two. This is Jayme's time to be free just before she leaves for the graveyard shift at Liberty Manor. Neal answers.

How's it going?" Jayme asks.

"Pretty good. Two tests tomorrow. How's it going with you?"

"B-minus on an English essay on Beowulf. It's like a comic book."

"Hope you didn't say that on Rodgers' test."

"No indeed. I went into the advantages of tearing off the arms of enemies."

"I know old Rodgers went for that."

"He must have. Anyway a B-minus is not bad."

"Did you hear or see about the blood-stained khakis and shirt in the dump over in the Whitsville landfill?"

"Scott's you mean?"

"Yeah."

"That's what we think. Son said there might be more to it than the paper said."

"I'm sure. I'm just glad Scott's gone. I heard the turquoise earring was in the shirt pocket."

"That's bad, to be young and people hope you're dead."

"Can you come up next weekend to the concert?"

"I wondered when you were going to ask!"

"Well, your B-minus means that you have some potential."

"Think yew. You mean I can be your true love. Your BFF and more."

"But not with privileges yet? You're still in that Platonic phase? Don't answer. Say hello to all your family for me."

"I will and I am glad about coming to the concert and of course, seeing you."

"Abyssinia."

"Samoa."

Helen wants Jayme to come to the Briarview for the Saturday night Real Estate banquet. She says it will be special and Gram says she should go. Gram loves Helen, and Son has always said he loves the part of Helen that he used to love, if that made any sense. Not much, but it sounds nicer than when Son talks about the parts of Helen he couldn't stand. Helen has been given six awards for closing land deals that will enhance the community the most, offering the clients the most services, the Golden Contract Award, and the Personality Award.

Jayme feels about thirty years old in the Vera dress, short and with pink and red flowers all over and her new soft leather sandals... "I got these for you when I was last in New York. Maybe your feet have stopped growing and you can wear these until you are thirty. Then you'll know what you want and, I'm sure, be able to get what you want." Helen is chattering at her all the way home.

"Mom, if you'll shut up, I mean, be quiet, I want to say something about all the speeches they made about you. The awards and all. You'll make the million-dollar circle one day, just like your grandfather."

"I didn't know you knew that." Helen was wiping the tears and mascara off her cheek bones—the ones she said she was lucky to have inherited from Great Aunt Alice.

"These are good tears, not sad ones. You have such a wonderful family behind you. Not just mine, but Son's too, even though we can't live together. I hope you know I still love Son, and even his ridiculous farm, or whatever you call it. And of course, as you know, to repeat myself, we can't live together."

"I'm beginning to understand more all the time. I think I have a thing for old people. I used to hope Gram would break her neck when she came down the steps or that Joe would blow himself up in the shed. Now I don't. I can live with them. And with myself—well, most of the time."

"Not to be too mushy, I'd like to thank you for what you've just said about the awards. I know that I seem shallow and 'wired' to you and Son. Jimmy knew it was just an act of mine and your Gram knows it on her good days. Joe does too."

The next Saturday driving Monticello Mountain to see Neal, Jayme feels like a real person. To get in the mood, as Jimmy used to say, she has the two six packs of Bud under her knees on the floor and radio as loud as it can go. Alabama is singing "Mountain Music" and the highway is going up into the mountains. Jayme can't believe she is as happy as she is. Maybe Gram is right about sunshine and shadows adding up to all there is to life. Add music, a car, Son's collectible, the 1952 BMW, not the Yukon she had thought he'd offer her, and Neal waiting for her but not expecting more than the usual.

Maybe Scott is making it in Colorado, pretending to be a real, registered student, but looking for a deal to put together or pull off, paid for in pills or term papers.

Joe was sitting out in the boxwoods when Jayme had left. "Have some for me," he'd said.

"I will," Jayme had answered, feeling like Joe was treating her like he had Jimmy.

"How much, Joe?" she asked.

"As much as you can take and still drive your Dad's BMW without wrecking it. We've been there and do not need to go again."

"Yes, sir," Jayme had said, and grabbed Joe's hand. "Let me feel your grip. You got any grip left?" Joe had squeezed as hard as he could, but it wasn't as burning and strong as it was two weeks ago.

"Don't ruin my driving hand," she'd said. Joe smiled and lit a Chesterfield regular from the one he was finishing.

Then Jayme had gone to find Gram who against Son's orders was trying not to go to sleep and was acting out picking dried black-eyed peas hanging like fingers, yellow bones, from the dry vines in the garden. Jayme knew this little game and could play it with Gram.

"Son better not know you're out here getting too hot and tired." Jayme tried to pretend walk her Gram back toward the house as she lay down with her for a few minutes.

"You won't tell him, will you, Jayme, that we are out in the garden? And besides, as Uncle Bootsie used to say, 'Don't make no never mind, anyways.' Which means in my case, I am beyond being careful. I'm free of all that, my Jayme Bird." Gram had smiled so sweetly at Jayme, her silvery hair shining in the night light, that she had felt her Gram's freedom, and wonderfully, her own.

"I'll see you when I get back and tell you all about it."

"I'll be waiting for you, Jayme."

Gram was trying to bend down from being flat on her back so she would not miss grabbing the cluster of skeleton-like peas, dry and crackling on the vines.

The next day on the highway, Jayme turns up the music, pounds on the steering wheel, opens the window and yells out into the rushing cold air, "Hello, Big Hills, I'm Jayme!"

ABOUT THE AUTHOR

Susan Pepper Robbins is a writing instructor at Hampden-Sydney College. Her previous works have been awarded the Deep South Prize and the Virginia Prize and include *One Way Home* and the story collection *Nothing but the Weather*. She lives in rural Virginia.

ABOUT THE PRESS

Unsolicited Press is based out of Portland, Oregon and focuses on the works of the unsung and underrepresented. As a womxn-owned, all-volunteer small publisher that doesn't worry about profits as much as championing exceptional literature, we have the privilege of partnering with authors skirting the fringes of the lit world. We've worked with emerging and award-winning authors such as Shann Ray, Amy Shimshon-Santo, Brook Bhagat, Kris Amos, and John W. Bateman.

Learn more at unsolicitedpress.com. Find us on twitter and instagram.

Printed in the USA
CPSIA information can be obtained
at www.ICGtesting.com
LVHW091759261123
764962LV00048B/943